GW00383523

*Have you been
invited to all these
sleepovers?*

Sleepover Girls and Friends

by Narinder Dhami

Collins

An Imprint of HarperCollinsPublishers

The Sleepover Club ® is a
registered trademark of HarperCollins*Publishers* Ltd

First published in Great Britain by Collins in 1999
Collins is an imprint of HarperCollins*Publishers* Ltd
77-85 Fulham Palace Road, Hammersmith,
London, W6 8JB

The HarperCollins website address is
www.fireandwater.com

1 3 5 7 9 8 6 4 2

Text copyright © Narinder Dhami 1999

Original series characters, plotlines
and settings © Rose Impey 1997

ISBN 0 00675423-6

The author asserts the moral right to
be identified as the author of the work.

Printed and bound in Great Britain by
Caledonian International Book Manufacturing Ltd,
Glasgow G64

Conditions of Sale
This book is sold subject to the condition
that it shall not, by way of trade or otherwise,
be lent, re-sold, hired out or otherwise circulated
without the publisher's prior consent in any form,
binding or cover other than that in which it is
published and without a similar condition
including this condition being imposed
on the subsequent purchaser.

Sleepover Kit List

1. Sleeping bag
2. Pillow
3. Pyjamas or a nightdress
4. Slippers
5. Toothbrush, toothpaste, soap etc
6. Towel
7. Teddy
8. A creepy story
9. Food for a midnight feast:
   chocolate, crisps, sweets, biscuits.
   In fact anything you like to eat.
10. Torch
11. Hairbrush
12. Hair things like a bobble or hairband,
    if you need them
13. Clean knickers and socks
14. Change of clothes for the next day
15. Sleepover diary and membership card

CHAPTER ONE

SURPRISE! It's me, Kenny. It's my turn to tell you what's been happening to us recently, and boy, have I got a story to tell you! You just won't believe it!

You remember the Sleepover Club, don't you? As if you could forget! There's five of us – me (I'm the wild one), Frankie (the sensible one – well, sometimes), Lyndz (the Hiccup Queen), Fliss (who can be a bit of a fusspot) and Rosie (who's a lot happier since we decorated her bedroom for her – but that's another story). We've had our Sleepover Club going for ages now. It's Top Secret, but we don't mind our friends like *you* knowing all about what we get up to.

But when all this started, we weren't getting up to much anyway. In fact, we were all feeling pretty down...

"I'm fed up with all this rain!" I moaned as we trailed back into school when the lunch hour was over. "I wish it was summer."

"Yeah, so do I," said Fliss. "EEEK!"

Ryan Scott, who's in our class, had just gone past and flicked his wet scarf at her.

"He fancies you, Fliss!" Frankie remarked, winking at me.

Fliss turned pink. "Oh, don't be silly!" she said, but you know what Fliss is like. She's had a thing about Ryan Scott for ages.

"I don't think we're going on holiday this year," Frankie sighed. "Not with the baby and all that." (Frankie's mum's having a baby, remember?)

"Nor are we," Lyndz added gloomily, "but my gran and grandpa might be coming to stay with us."

"My dad *says* he's going to pay for us to go

on holiday," Rosie muttered, "but I'll believe that when I see it!" (Rosie's dad says a lot of stuff, but he doesn't always get round to doing it.)

"Did I tell you—" Fliss began eagerly.

"Yeah, about fifty million times!" I said, taking off my coat.

Fliss looked offended. "You don't even know what I'm going to say!"

"I'll take a guess." I grinned at her. "*We're going to Majorca and it's going to be great!*"

Fliss had nearly sent us all bananas going on and on about her holiday to Majorca. Secretly though, I was a bit jealous. My mum and dad love going to places like Scotland and Wales, and although I like being out of doors, I don't mind a bit of sun either.

"Well, it *is* going to be great!" Fliss said crossly. "I can't wait!"

"Remember when we went to Spain?" Frankie said as we trooped into the classroom. "That was brilliant!"

We all looked out of the classroom window at the rain coming down in sheets and felt even more miserable. That school trip to Spain was everyone's best holiday *ever*. The weather had been scorching, the beaches were fab and best of all we'd made friends with five Spanish girls called Pilar, Maria, Isabella, Elena and Anna. At first we'd hated each other – that was sort of my fault. OK, it *was* my fault. But then we'd got over it and had a brilliant time together. We'd told the girls all about our Sleepover Club and they'd started one for themselves. Since we'd got back from Spain we'd kept in touch by emailing them every week from our class computer.

"Come on everyone, sit down quickly." Mrs Weaver came in, glancing round the room and glaring at anyone whose bottom wasn't firmly on a seat. "Emma and Emily, didn't you hear what I said?"

"Sorry, Miss," Emma Hughes said in a sugary-sweet voice. "Emily and I thought the bookshelves were looking a bit messy, so we were just tidying them up."

"Oh, thank you, girls," said Mrs Weaver.

I just looked at the other Sleepovers and

pulled a face like I was about to be sick. The M&Ms *always* have that effect on me!

The M&Ms, in case you've been asleep for the last zillion years and don't remember, are our *biggest* enemies. They're also known as the Queen and the Goblin because Emma Hughes just thinks she's so cool, and Emily Berryman's small and has got this really gruff voice. We totally hate them, and they hate us. Oh hang on a sec, I didn't tell you what happened at Katie's party last week, did I? It was so coo-ell!

Katie Dawson, who's in our class, had a birthday party last week and she invited just about everyone, including us and the M&Ms. It was a really brill party with loud music and masses of food. Katie's mum had ordered loads of pizzas from the pizza place in the High Street, so we were all well pleased.

Then the M&Ms had to go and spoil it by putting a piece of squishy tomato on Fliss's chair. So when Fliss sat down on it, it stuck to the white jeans she was wearing and ruined them. Fliss went totally ballistic, so I decided it was time for the Sleepover Club to get their revenge.

I strolled over to the M&Ms, as cool as anything.

"Looks like Fliss has had a bit of an accident!" Emily was chortling in that stupid deep voice of hers.

"Yeah, Fliss, you're supposed to eat tomato, not wear it!" Emma called, laughing her head off.

"Talking of wearing things, Emma," I said, grabbing the nearest pizza from the table, "is this your size?"

And I turned the plate over and dropped the pizza on to Emma's head. Toppings side down.

Oh, *what* a laugh that was! Emma just sat there open-mouthed for a second or two. Then all this cheese and tomato and onion started dripping down her face. The other Sleepovers were in hysterics.

'Course, we all got told off and sent home, but it was totally worth it just to see the look on Emma's face! Anyway, now the M&Ms hate us more than ever, and they're sure to try and get back at us somehow. We've got to watch our backs for a bit.

"Right, I've got some good news for you," Mrs Weaver said, after she'd taken the register. "It's particularly good news for those of you who went on the school trip to Spain a while back."

We all sat up, ears flapping.

"I've been in touch with the teachers of some of the Spanish students we met while we were over there," Mrs Weaver went on. "And we've arranged for eleven of the pupils to come over to visit Cuddington in July."

The Sleepover Club started nudging each other and whispering. What we all wanted to know was, were our friends going to be coming over on that trip or not? So I put my hand up.

"Yes, Laura?"

"Miss, are those girls we made friends with coming?" I asked.

Mrs Weaver asked their names, then checked the piece of paper in her hand. "Yes, they're all down on the list."

I turned to the others. "*Ex-cellent!*"

"It'll be great to see them all again!" Rosie gasped.

"I can feel a gi-normous sleepover coming on!" Frankie whispered.

"Quiet for a moment, please," Mrs Weaver said, glancing over at us. "The students and their teachers will be arriving on Friday July 12th and staying until the end of the summer term, Tuesday 23rd. I know it's only April now, but we have to find them places to stay. If anyone would like one of the Spanish pupils to board with them, please take one of these letters home tonight, and see me tomorrow morning *after* you've checked with your parents."

We were all getting pretty excited now. It would just be *so* cool having our Spanish friends staying with us! I really hoped that Maria would want to come and stay with me – we could talk about football all night!

"Right, get out your books for silent reading, please," Mrs Weaver told us.

Everyone started talking then, and we all

got our books out as slowly as possible so we had more time to natter about what Mrs W. had just told us.

"They're coming at the end of the summer term – that's *brill*!" Lyndz exclaimed. "There's always loads of stuff going on then!"

"Yeah, there's Sports Day and the Summer Fete," I pointed out.

"And we'll hopefully get a class trip to WonderLand, that fab new theme park!" Frankie added.

"Oh, and don't forget the fancy-dress competition on the last day of term!" Fliss squealed.

Rosie was looking a bit put out. "Yeah," she said pointedly, "and there's something else too!"

"What?" I asked, but Frankie nudged me in the ribs.

"It's Rosie's birthday, of course!" she hissed.

"Oh, right, July 15th!" I grinned. "What about an extra-special sleepover?"

Rosie was beaming all over her face by now. "That'd be excellent!"

It was then that I noticed the M&Ms standing by the bookshelves near our table, looking seriously grumpy.

"Oh, I forgot!" I said loudly. "*Some* people in this class weren't lucky enough to go on the school trip to Spain!"

The Queen had had chickenpox at the time and the Goblin didn't want to go without her, so now we could *really* rub their noses in it!

The M&Ms flounced off, looking annoyed, and left us all giggling.

"I can't *wait* for July!" I said. "It's going to be seriously brilliant!"

But I didn't know just how wrong I was...

CHAPTER TWO

"Quick, check the email box, Kenny!" Fliss poked me hard in the back. "See if Isabella and the others have replied to our last email!"

"OK, OK!" I said crossly, as the others crowded round me eagerly. "Stop hassling me!"

It was a few days after Mrs Weaver had told us about the Spanish pupils coming to visit. It was mine and Lyndz's turn to use the class computer, and, although we were supposed to be finishing off the story we were writing together, Mrs W. had agreed to let us check the email box and send a reply.

"We've got an answer!" Frankie announced triumphantly as a new message popped up on the screen. "Quick, Kenny, see what they say!"

I hit the mouse, and opened the message.

```
Hi, Sleepover Club!
We look forward very much to see
you all in England in July. We
are all very excited. Can we have
a special sleepover when we are
staying with you?
   Love from Pilar, Maria,
Isabella, Elena and Anna
```

"Go on, Kenny!" This time it was Rosie who poked me in the back. "Tell them it's my birthday, and we're going to have a big sleepover on the day they arrive!"

Frankie tapped me on the shoulder. "Tell them we're going to sleep out in a tent in Rosie's garden if the weather's good!"

"And tell them they're going to be staying with us!" Lyndz added, jogging my elbow.

"Will you lot get off!" I moaned. "I'm going to be black and blue all over at this rate!" And I started typing in our reply.

Dear Spanish Sleepover Club,
We're really excited too, and we
can't wait for July! We've got
loads of exciting stuff happening
here. First, it's Rosie's
birthday a few days after you get
here, so we're going to have a
big birthday sleepover on the day
you arrive! We'll have a party in
Rosie's garden, and then we're
going to sleep out in a big tent.
We're going to play loads of
games, give each other makeovers,
have a fashion show and stuff our
faces with birthday food!

"No pizzas though!" Fliss said as I typed that,
and we all started laughing.

"I heard that!" snapped Emma Hughes, who
was sitting nearby. "And it wasn't funny!"

"Oh yes, it was!" I retorted wickedly. "Seeing
you with tomato sauce sliding down your face
would make anyone laugh!"

"You think you're so clever, Laura

McKenzie!" Emily Berryman chimed in.

"Well, at least I'm not stupid enough to wear a pizza on my head!" I pointed out, and the other Sleepovers fell about.

"Take no notice of them, Emma," said Emily.

"I won't," Emma said, and stuck her nose in the air.

"Wait till our Spanish friends get here!" Frankie said gleefully. "Then there'll be *ten* of us to get on your nerves!"

"These Spanish girls must be crazy," Emma sniffed. "Fancy wanting to be mates with a bunch of losers like you!"

I nudged Frankie. "Emma's looking just a little bit green, don't you think?"

"Oh, definitely," Frankie agreed. "She's starting to go green all over!"

"I am *not* jealous!" Emma snorted furiously. "I don't care if you've got a *million* Spanish friends!"

"So how many Spanish people do *you* know, Emma?" Fliss asked.

Emma picked up her work and stormed across the classroom to queue up at Mrs

Weaver's table. Emily followed, leaving us all in fits of giggles.

"This visit is really winding the M&Ms up!" Frankie said.

"Good!" I replied. "They deserve it!"

"Come on Kenny, get on with the email," Lyndz said. "Mrs Weaver keeps giving us dirty looks."

Quickly I began to type again:

```
Has your teacher told you you're
going to be staying with us?
Pilar's staying with Frankie,
Isabella with Fliss, Elena with
Lyndz, Anna with Rosie and Maria
with me. So you and me can have
lots of arguments about footy,
Maria!
   Got to go now, because our
teacher's giving us dirty looks!
REPLY SOON.
   Kenny, Lyndz, Frankie, Rosie
and Fliss
```

"It's funny how you and Maria both like football, Kenny," Frankie remarked as I sent the email on its way to sunny Spain. "And you're both a bit mad too."

"Well, what about you and Pilar?" I retorted. "You're both about six feet tall and bossy with it!"

We'd discovered that the Spanish girls were so much like us, it was spooky. Isabella and Fliss were scarily alike – they'd even had exactly the same swimsuits on holiday! Elena and Anna, who were twins, were a bit like Lyndz and Rosie too. Elena was pretty easy-going, like Lyndz, and she was always getting hiccups too! And Anna was kind-hearted, but she could be a bit prickly sometimes (sound like anyone you know?). Anyway, the reason why we got on so well with them was probably because we *were* so alike.

"How many days to wait before they get here?" I asked.

"Seventy-five," Frankie said immediately. "I worked it out last night."

"Seventy-five days!" I groaned. "That's ages!

We might be dead by then!"

Frankie gave me a shove. "Oh, look on the bright side, Kenny, why don't you!"

"Anyway, it gives us lots of time to plan what we're going to do," Lyndz added.

"Yeah, this has got to be special!" I said firmly. "We want to make sure Pilar and the others have a trip they'll never forget!"

* * *

"Are they here yet?" Fliss asked for about the millionth time, standing up to peer out of the classroom window.

"Not unless they're invisible, and so is their coach!" I said impatiently. "I'll tell you as soon as I see them."

It was Friday July 12th at *last*. It seemed a very long time since Mrs Weaver had first told us that the Spanish pupils were coming over, but at last the day had arrived. They were coming to our school from the airport by coach, and because I had the best view of the playground gates from my seat, I was watching out for them. We were all supposed to be doing silent reading, but Mrs Weaver wasn't bothering much about keeping us quiet. She was pretty cool about things now that we were almost at the end of term.

"I hope it doesn't rain tonight," Rosie said anxiously, glancing out of the window. "Not now we've decorated the garden and put the tent up."

The rest of us looked at each other and giggled. The sun was blazing into the classroom – there'd been a heatwave for the last two weeks and the weather was *scorching*. It was even hotter than it was when we'd gone to Spain.

"It's going to be brill sleeping outside tonight!" I said. We'd spent the last few days round at Rosie's after school, getting everything ready for the Grand Sleepover that evening. Although the Cartwrights' garden, like their house, was a bit of a mess, we'd hung streamers and balloons in the trees, and my dad had brought our big tent over and put it up on the grass.

"Yeah, but no horror stories, Kenny, all right?" Fliss insisted nervously.

"Nah, 'course not!" I said, crossing my fingers behind my back and winking at Frankie. I had a fab story to tell at the sleepover that night, all about a mummy, a werewolf and a haunted house. Fliss was going to wet herself!

"I wonder why Pilar and the others didn't reply to that email we sent them the other day?" Lyndz said.

Frankie shrugged. "Maybe their teacher wouldn't let them."

We hadn't heard anything from the Spanish girls for nearly two weeks now.

"Maybe they were too busy getting ready for the trip," I suggested. "Hey, here's the coach!"

Everyone in the classroom jumped out of their seats and rushed over to the windows, except the M&Ms. Typical. Meanwhile, Mrs Weaver had grabbed her clipboard and hurried outside.

"There's Maria!" I yelled, as the Spanish kids

began to file off the coach, looking a bit tired and crumpled. Maria was at the front, wearing her Real Madrid football shirt as usual. I banged on the glass and waved. "MARIA!"

Maria glanced over, but she didn't wave back.

"I guess she just didn't see me," I said, disappointed.

"There's Pilar!" Frankie began to bang on the glass too, but Pilar wasn't taking any notice either. Neither were Isabella, Elena and Anna, who got off behind her.

"Maybe they don't like you any more!" remarked Emma Hughes with a spiteful grin, but we ignored her.

We watched Mrs Weaver leading the Spanish kids and their two teachers into school, and then they came into our classroom.

"Hey, Maria!" I shouted, trying to attract her attention, but I had to shut up when Mrs W. gave me one of her mega-gruesome glares.

"Sit down, everyone, please!" she called. *"Quietly!"*

Although we couldn't say anything, we kept on grinning and giving Pilar, Maria and the others thumbs-up signs. But it was really strange because they weren't doing anything back. In fact, they were acting as if they didn't even know who we were. They were staring straight through us.

"What's going on?" I whispered to Frankie. "Why're they being so funny?"

Frankie shrugged. "Maybe they're just tired after the flight," she suggested.

"What, too tired to *smile* at us?" I said.

I stared hard at Maria until I caught her eye. You know what she did? She just stared right back at me. She didn't smile. She didn't wink. She didn't do anything. It was really strange.

There was *definitely* something very weird going on. And I was determined to find out exactly what it was...

CHAPTER THREE

"And this is where you'll be sleeping!" I threw open the door of my bedroom, and grinned at Maria. "My sister Molly the Monster's gone to camp with her school, so you'll be sharing with me. Cool, huh?"

Maria didn't say anything. Which wasn't surprising really because she'd hardly said a word to me at all. We hadn't had much time to chat at school because the home bell had rung about fifteen minutes after the coach had arrived, and then my mum turned up in the car to drive us home. I could see the other Sleepovers looking just as puzzled as I was, as they went off with their mum or dad and the Spanish girl who was staying with them. It was *weird*.

I'd been mega-nice to Maria in the car when my mum took us home, but she'd hardly said a word to me. I'd told her all about the special sleepover at Rosie's and even that hadn't made any difference. She was fine when my mum spoke to her though! And that had really got right up my nose. I was getting seriously annoyed.

"Come on," I said, still trying to be nice. "Let's go and kick a ball around in the garden or something."

"No, thanks." Maria shrugged. "I want to unpack my suitcase."

"OK," I said. "Do you want some help?"

"Not from you!" Maria retorted rudely, and I almost choked with fury.

"What's *that* supposed to mean?"

"It means I not want you to help me!" Maria glared at me, and that just about did it. I was *boiling*.

"You're really starting to get on my nerves!"

I hissed, clenching my fists. "What's going on?"

"Why you ask *me* what is going on?" Maria snapped. We were standing nose-to-nose now like a couple of heavyweight boxers. "*You* start it!"

"Start what?" I asked, bewildered. I totally didn't have a clue what she was going on about.

Maria looked like she was about to say something, but then she just stuck her tongue out at me. If Molly the Monster had done that to me I'd have grabbed my pillow and whacked her round the head with it, but somehow I managed to stop myself. Instead I stomped out of the room, leaving Maria unpacking her suitcase.

I just couldn't understand what was going on. Up until a week or two ago we'd all been great mates. So what had gone wrong?

When I got downstairs, I picked up the phone and called Frankie.

"Hey, Franks, how's it's going?"

"Gruesome!" Frankie groaned. "Pilar's being a right pain!"

"So's Maria," I agreed. "Did Pilar tell you why they're acting like total morons?"

"Nah, she won't even *talk* to me!" Frankie said in disgust. "I just phoned Lyndz and she said Elena's being just as weird!"

"Right, I'll phone Fliss and you phone Rosie," I decided. "Somehow we've got to find out what's going on, or the next few weeks are going to be a total disaster!"

"Isabella's driving me bananas!" Fliss complained when I got through to her. "She keeps on making nasty remarks about my teddy-bear collection – she says hers is much better!"

"Never mind that!" I said impatiently. "Has she told you why they're all being so weird?"

"No," Fliss replied. "I just phoned Rosie and she says that Anna won't tell her either."

"Well, maybe we'll find out at the sleepover tonight..."

I said goodbye to Fliss, and put the phone down. I was beginning to wonder if the Grand Sleepover we'd planned so carefully was going to be quite so grand after all...

*   *   *

"Er – shall we start the sleepover now?" Rosie asked, looking round at us.

We all nodded silently. Rosie opened the French windows that led out of the Cartwrights' living-room into the garden, and we all trudged gloomily after her. What a great evening this was going to be. Since we'd all arrived at Rosie's place, no-one had said a word to each other. We'd all just sat on the sofas, the Sleepover Club on one and the Spanish girls on another, and we'd glared across the room at each other. Rosie was already looking pretty hassled, and I didn't blame her. This was supposed to be her birthday sleepover, and by the look of it, it was going to be about as jolly as a three-hour maths test.

"Oh, hello girls." Rosie's mum was laying out loads of food on a table which had been set up near the tent. "I bet you're looking forward to this, aren't you?"

Nobody said anything. Mrs Cartwright took

one look at our faces, blinked and then decided not to say anything.

"Have a good time!" she called as she went back to the house.

Yeah, right. We were *really* going to enjoy ourselves when everyone was walking around with their faces down to their knees. Well, it looked like it was up to me to get this party going a bit!

"OK, what shall we do first?" I asked loudly, making everyone jump. "Shall we play International Gladiators?"

"Nah, let's eat!" said Lyndz.

"We could give Rosie her presents first," Frankie suggested.

"No, let's have makeovers first!" Fliss chimed in. "I've borrowed some make-up from my mum."

"Yes, I think makeover is a good idea!" Pilar said suddenly. She looked at the other Spanish girls, who nodded.

"Yeah, OK," I agreed. I'm definitely not into trying out hairstyles and make-up like Flissy is – I was just trying to be friendly.

"We give you makeovers first!" Isabella announced, grabbing the make-up bag Fliss had just taken out of her rucksack. "We make you look beautiful!"

Frankie had brought some make-up and nail varnish too, as well as brushes and combs, and Rosie ran into the house to get some mirrors. Then we started the makeovers. Maria was doing mine, and although I told her not to use too much make-up because I didn't like it, it felt like she was using *tons* of it.

"What are you doing, Maria?" I asked, trying to twist round a bit so that I could get a look at the others.

"Keep still!" Maria grabbed my arm and pulled me round to face her again. "I cannot make it right if you move!"

"Hey, that tickles!" I heard Frankie complaining. "What's that, Pilar?"

"I use lipliner and lipstick," Pilar said. "Now stay quiet!"

The other Spanish girls started giggling, and that made me a bit suspicious. Then we heard barking, and Adam came into the garden with three of his mates and his dog Jenny. Adam's got cerebral palsy and he's in a wheelchair. He can talk, sort of, but mostly he uses a computerised voicebox.

"Hey Adam," I called. "You all right?"

Adam stopped in his chair and stared at us. Then he and his mates all started to roar with laughter.

"Maria, what've you done?" I yelled, grabbing one of the mirrors.

I had *loads* of black eyeliner slapped on all round my eyes and a big red mouth. I looked like Bobo the clown! And the others weren't any better.

"Look at me!" Frankie gasped. Pilar had drawn a pair of glasses and a fake moustache on her face with eyeliner!

"My hair!" Fliss wailed, grabbing a mirror. "What've you done to my hair?" Isabella had backcombed it so that it was all frizzy and looked like a bird's nest.

"I look stupid!" Rosie spluttered. She had enough blusher on her cheeks to sink the

Titanic, and her hair had been gelled into spikes which stuck up all over her head. She looked gruesome.

"I look like I've got the measles!" Lyndz howled, glaring at Elena, who'd put little black spots of eyeliner pencil all over her face.

"Right, that's it!" I leapt to my feet, rubbing hard at the make-up with a tissue. "You lot are dead!"

Maria and the others were rolling on the grass, crying with laughter.

"It serve you right!" Isabella said triumphantly.

"You should not send us those emails!" Pilar added. "Now we pay you back!"

"What are you talking about?" I stared at them. "What emails?"

"You know what we talk about!" Maria said scornfully. She put her hand in her bag and pulled out some papers. "*These* emails!"

She shoved them into my hand and I read the one on top, which was dated a week or so ago.

```
Dear Spanish girls
Why don't you learn how to talk
English properly?
  Kenny, Frankie, Rosie, Lyndz
and Fliss
```

"You say other things too," Elena said. "Nasty things about our country!"

"Yes, we are proud to be Spanish!" Anna added fiercely.

"We didn't send these!" I said, showing them to the other Sleepovers. "No way!"

"We've never seen them before!" Frankie backed me up, and the others nodded.

Maria and the other girls obviously didn't believe us. "So who send them then?" Maria asked.

I looked at the others. "I bet I know who it was!" I hissed. "I bet it was—"

"Kenny!" Maria called, and I spun round.

"AARGH!"

A cream doughnut hit me right in the middle of my face!

CHAPTER FOUR

Well, that was IT! I wasn't in the mood to try and sort things out any more – this was WAR!

"You shouldn't have done that!" I spluttered as I wiped cream and sugar off my face while the Spanish girls roared with laughter. "You're really going to get it now!"

"Kenny, be careful!" said Fliss and Lyndz together, but I was too mad to listen. I grabbed a cheese and pickle roll off the table and threw it at Maria. She ducked, but it hit Pilar instead, and Branston pickle spilled out all over her jeans.

"Hey!" Pilar shouted, "you dirty my jeans!"

And she scooped some cream off the top of the trifle with a spoon, and flicked it at us. It hit Fliss right in the eye.

"Ow!" Fliss wailed, and she lobbed a ham roll in the Spanish girls' direction.

Next second it had turned into a free-for-all as we all started grabbing food missiles and hurling them at each other.

"Stop it!" Rosie yelled. "You're ruining my birthday sleepover!"

Then she got a sausage roll in the eye, and that made her so mad, she started to join in. It was like something out of a comedy film. Everyone was screaming and trying to dodge flying cakes and rolls, Jenny was barking madly and Adam and his friends were all watching us and laughing their heads off.

I hadn't managed to land a direct hit on Maria yet, so I spooned some strawberry jelly into a bowl, and flung it in her direction. I didn't get Maria. But I did manage to get Rosie's mum. Right in the middle of her face!

"Well!" Mrs Cartwright stared furiously at us, trying to wipe strawberry jelly out of her eyes. She must have come out to see what all the noise was about, and we'd been so busy fighting, we hadn't heard her. "What on *earth* is going on here?"

"Er – we were having a food fight, Mum," Rosie muttered sheepishly, while the rest of us shuffled our feet and tried to brush the crumbs out of our hair.

"I can see *that*," Mrs Cartwright replied in a freezing tone. "I think you'd better clear everything up straightaway. And then I'm going to ring your parents and you're all going home."

"What about the sleepover?" Rosie wailed, but her mum just gave her a look that shut her up.

"*You* started that!" I hissed at Maria when Mrs Cartwright had gone back into the house. "This is all your fault!"

Maria shrugged. "You start it with all your nasty emails!"

"We didn't send them!" I began, but I could see it was no use. They just didn't believe us.

Rosie was looking really upset. "This has

been my worst birthday ever!" she groaned. "And it isn't even my birthday till Monday!"

"Never mind, you've still got your prezzies to look forward to," said Lyndz.

"Mum's so mad with me, I probably won't get *anything*!" Rosie muttered.

"What're we going to do now?" Frankie asked as we began to pick up squashed cakes and rolls from the grass and put them into bin bags. The Spanish girls started clearing up too, but they kept well away from us, and they were whispering to each other and giving us filthy looks.

"We're just going to have to prove to them that it wasn't us who sent those emails!" I said.

"How?" asked Lyndz.

"We need to find out who sent them," I said. "And I've got a pretty good idea who it was too…"

*　　*　　*

"Right, hands up everyone who thinks it was the gruesome M&Ms who sent those emails!" I announced.

Everyone's hand immediately went up, and I grinned.

"Yeah, so do I!" I agreed. "So what're we going to do about it?"

It was the day after the not-so-Grand Sleepover, and Frankie, Lyndz, Fliss and Rosie were round at my place to discuss exactly what we were going to do. We'd all been well and truly roasted alive by our parents when we got home after the food fight, and Pilar and the others had been told off by their teacher, Miss Moreno. We'd also been told that we couldn't have a sleepover next weekend. For once, we didn't care that much though. It wouldn't have been any fun with Maria and the rest of her Gruesome Gang!

"I tried to talk to Elena last night," said Lyndz, "but she was still in a right mood."

"Yeah, Anna was too," Rosie agreed. "She even asked my mum if she could sleep in a different bedroom instead of sharing with me!"

"Well, Isabella wouldn't speak to me either," Fliss chimed in. "*And* she snores!"

"I got the big freeze from Pilar too," Frankie

said. "What about you, Kenny?"

"I tried talking to Maria when we went to bed," I said. "But she wouldn't listen. She put her headphones on so she couldn't hear me, and she had her Walkman on really loudly!"

"They're really mad with us," said Rosie. "Those emails must have been pretty bad."

"I could murder the M&Ms!" I muttered. "They're not gonna get away with this!"

"We'll have to have another go at talking to Pilar and the others," I said. "What time do they get back from Leicester?"

"They should be back pretty soon," Lyndz replied. Miss Moreno and Mr Cortez, the Spanish teachers, had come round in a minibus that morning and collected the pupils to take them to Leicester on a shopping trip. "Then they're going to the park for a picnic."

"Right, let's get over there then and tell them about the M&Ms!" I jumped to my feet. "We'll make them believe us even if we have to sit on their heads and bounce up and down on them!"

"Oh, right, like *that* can't fail!" Frankie said

sarcastically. "They'll *really* want to be friends with us after that!"

"Just keep cool, will you Kenny!" Fliss said nervously. "We don't want to start another fight!"

I gave her a shove. "That wasn't my fault, it was Maria's. You know me, I'm just not the fighting type!"

The park wasn't far away from my place, and we were allowed to go to it on our own, so we set off.

"We ought to start thinking about making our fancy-dress costumes soon," Lyndz remarked. "We've only got a week and a bit to get them ready."

We always have a fancy-dress competition at school on the last day of the summer term, which is really wicked. Even the teachers dress up, and there's prizes for the best home-made costumes.

"I was just going to wear my Leicester City football strip," I began, but everyone else started groaning loudly.

"Bor-ing, Kenny!" said Frankie. "That's what

you've worn for the last three years!"

"My mum says she'll hire a costume for me," said Fliss. "It'll be a lot easier than making it."

"Even *more* bor-ing!" the rest of us said together.

"You've got to make it yourself or you can't win a prize," Lyndz added.

"I think I might go as an alien," Frankie said. "Then I can wear my cool new silver nail varnish."

"I could go as a clown," I suggested. "Then I could get Maria to do my make-up!"

The others started to laugh.

"You'd probably frighten the kids in the Infants to death!" Fliss pointed out.

"I wonder if Maria and the others are going to dress up too?" Rosie said. "They're going to be there on the last day of term, after all."

"Maybe we could offer to help them with their costumes," Lyndz suggested.

"Yeah, that might be a good way of making friends with them again," Frankie agreed, as we arrived at the park.

"They're back from Leicester," said Lyndz.

"There's the minibus."

"All right," I said as we walked up to the park gates. "Now everyone just stay cool and calm. Nobody loses their temper, OK?"

"What're you telling us for, Kenny?" Fliss sniffed. "*You're* the one who's likely to thump them if they won't listen to us!"

"What a cheek!" I began indignantly, but then I stopped. I'd just caught sight of the Spanish pupils sitting around on the grass in groups, eating their picnic. Maria, Pilar, Elena, Anna and Isabella were sitting near the swings, surrounded by lots of carrier bags full of shopping. And they weren't on their own either. They were laughing and chatting and sharing their picnic... *with the gruesome M&Ms!*

CHAPTER FIVE

We all stood and stared at them. Honestly, we must have looked like a bunch of stunned goldfish, standing there with our mouths open! The Spanish girls and the M&Ms didn't notice us though because they were too busy having a laugh together. It was unbelievable!

"They're making friends with the M&Ms!" Rosie gasped. "They must be crazy!"

"What're the M&Ms doing here anyway?" Lyndz asked.

"Who cares!" I was burning with fury. "They're here, and they're trying to get in with our mates! I'm going over to tell them exactly

47

what I think of them!"

"No, Kenny!" Frankie grabbed one of my arms and Lyndz clutched at the other. "You'll just make things worse!"

When I get mad though, there's no talking to me! I pushed Frankie and Lyndz off and stormed across the grass towards Maria and the others. They glanced up and saw me coming, and they started to laugh and nudge each other. Meanwhile the Queen and the Goblin looked so smug, I could have pushed them both into the boating lake.

"What do you want?" Maria snapped. "Go away, we try to eat our picnic."

"I want to talk to you!" I retorted. "About those emails!" I saw Emma Hughes flash a grin at Emily Berryman when I said that, and that wound me up even more. "If you want to know who sent them, just take a look over *there*!" And I pointed at the M&Ms.

"Oh, stop being a pain, Kenny, and go and play in the traffic!" said Emma Hughes with a pretend yawn. "Nobody wants to listen to you!"

Pilar and the other Spanish girls were all glaring at me. "Yes, go away, Kenny!" they chorused.

"We want to eat our picnic with our friends," said Maria pointedly.

Their friends! I almost choked. The M&Ms had done their best to split us up, and now they'd won and they were taking our mates away from us!

"You'd better tell them the truth, Emma Hughes!" I said threateningly, "or else!"

The Queen was beginning to look a bit worried by now, but just at that moment the other Sleepovers caught up with me and grabbed my arms again.

"Back off, Kenny!" Frankie hissed in my ear. "You're just making things worse!"

Even though I was mad, I could see what she meant. Pilar, Maria, Isabella, Elena and Anna just didn't believe what I was saying – not now that the M&Ms were being as nice as pie to them. I took a deep breath and tried to calm myself down.

"Look, we just want to talk to you," I said.

"Well, we not want to talk to *you*," said Elena, and the others nodded in agreement.

" 'Bye, Kenny!" said Emily Berryman with an infuriating grin.

"Come on, Kenny," Frankie whispered. "We don't want to talk to them with the Gruesome Twosome here anyway!"

"Yes, come on, Kenny!" Fliss tugged at my arm and took a step backwards. She accidentally trod on one of the bags of shopping lying on the grass, and there was a loud CRACK.

"My bag!" Isabella squealed. She pulled the carrier bag open, and took out an object wrapped in tissue paper. Inside was a pretty blue bowl. Well, it would have been a pretty bowl if it hadn't been in two pieces.

"I buy that for my mother!" Isabella yelled, her face turning red with fury. "Now you break it!"

"I didn't mean to," Fliss stammered.

"She did it on purpose!" Emma Hughes had to stick her nose in and try to stir things up as usual. "I saw her!"

"No, I didn't!" Fliss snapped. "You can shut up, Emma Hughes!"

"Make me!" Emma sneered.

"OK, if Fliss won't, I will!" I lunged forward, but Frankie caught my sleeve and dragged me back. She and the others hustled me away across the grass, leaving the Spanish girls furious and the M&Ms laughing.

"That Emma Hughes is *history*!" I snapped as Frankie and the others pulled me over to the park gates. "This mess is all down to her!"

"And now she's made friends with Anna and the others, they won't believe us if we try to tell them what she and Emily are *really* like," Rosie pointed out.

"No, I bet the Queen and the Goblin are being really nice to them!" I said, clenching my fists. "You know how two-faced Emma Hughes is!"

"Well, there's not much we can do about it, is there?" Frankie muttered, and nobody could think of anything to say.

We all trailed back miserably to my place, and went out into the garden. The sky was blue, the sun was shining, it was warm, and in just over a week's time we'd be finishing school for the summer holidays. But we couldn't help feeling fed up. We'd been looking forward to Pilar and the rest of the gang coming over so much, and now the M&Ms had gone and ruined it all.

"Why don't we design our fancy-dress costumes?" Lyndz asked.

No-one was that keen, but it was better than sitting around doing nothing. So I went inside and nicked some paper and pens from my dad's study, and then we lay around on the grass, sketching. I can't draw though, so I just doodled.

"I think I might go as the Tin Man," said Lyndz.

"What?" I glanced over at her.

"The Tin Man from *The Wizard of Oz*," Lyndz explained.

"That sounds like a hard costume to make," said Fliss.

"No, I'll just use loads of cardboard boxes and paint them silver," Lyndz said. "And I can make myself an oil-can to carry. It'll be great!"

"Well, I want to dress up in something glamorous!" said Fliss. "I don't want to be a rusty old Tin Man!"

"You could go as Barbie," I suggested, winking at Frankie. Fliss has got long fair hair, she's dead skinny and she's got about as many clothes as Barbie has! I meant it as a joke, but Fliss immediately looked interested.

"That's a good idea – then I wouldn't have to make a costume! I could just wear one of my dresses."

"I think I might go as the Witch from *The Lion, The Witch and The Wardrobe*," said Frankie. "Then I can still wear my silver nail varnish! What about you, Rosie?"

"I don't know," Rosie said gloomily, "I can't think of anything!"

"We'll help you," Lyndz told her.

"Hey, I've just had a great idea for my costume!" I said triumphantly. "And it's not my Leicester City strip either!"

I jumped to my feet and ran into the house. It took me a while to find what I was looking

53

for, but when I did, I took it outside.

"Remember *this*?" I said with a grin, holding it up.

"The mummy mask!" squealed Lyndz and Fliss together.

"I didn't know you'd still got that!" said Frankie.

Remember when went on that school trip to the museum and slept over, and we frightened the M&Ms to death with the mummy mask I'd made? That was just so cool!

"I'll go as a mummy!" I announced, putting the mask over my face. "All I've got to do is nick some bandages from my dad's surgery, and I'm sorted!"

"Maybe you can scare the M&Ms into telling the truth about those emails!" Lyndz suggested.

"Yeah, what are we going to do about that?" Rosie asked.

Everyone looked gloomy again.

"I wish I hadn't broken that bowl of Isabella's," Fliss sighed.

"If only there was some way we could prove

that the M&Ms sent those emails," Frankie said. "Then everything would be OK."

"And maybe I could buy Isabella another bowl," Fliss added.

"Well, we could find out what time the emails were sent by checking them," Lyndz pointed out. "But that doesn't help us very much because we can't prove who was using the computer at the time—"

"Lyndz!" I gasped, "you're a genius!"

Lyndz looked at me blankly. "I am?"

"Yeah, you are!" I said triumphantly. "We *can* prove who was using the class computer when those emails were sent!"

The others stared at me. They *still* didn't get it.

"Look," I gabbled impatiently, "how do we *always* know whose turn it is to use the computer?"

"Because Mrs Weaver puts a list up on the classroom noticeboard," Fliss replied.

"Exactly!" I grinned round at the others. "So all we've got to do is check out the list to see who got to use the computer and when last week, and compare it with the dates and times on the emails! Simple!"

"Kenny, you're brilliant!" gasped Frankie. "I'd like to see the M&Ms talk their way out of this one!"

"They won't be able to!" I said confidently. "We're going to prove to Maria and the others that the M&Ms are the bad guys – not us! I can't *wait* to see Emma Hughes' face on Monday morning!"

CHAPTER SIX

"Happy birthday to you,
Happy birthday to you,
You look like a monkey
And you smell like one too!"

"Thanks, Kenny!" Rosie gave me a shove as I finished singing and took a bow. "Now where's my prezzie?"

I dived into my schoolbag and pulled out a square-shaped parcel wrapped in Bacofoil. "Sorry, I forgot to get any wrapping-paper!" I grinned as I gave it to Rosie, and the others started giggling.

"Typical!" Rosie snorted, rolling her eyes.

It was Monday morning, and we'd all got to school early so we could give Rosie her presents. Everyone was pretending to be really jolly and up-for-it, but that was just because we didn't want Rosie's actual birthday to end up being more of a downer than it already was. The weekend had been pretty grim. Our sleepover had been ruined, we were in deepest doom with the Oldies because of the food fight and I was having to put up with sharing my bedroom with Maria, which was nearly as gruesome as sharing with Molly the Monster! Luckily the Spanish kids had been taken out again on Sunday by their teachers – they'd gone to visit some local museums, so at least we hadn't had to spend the day with them. We'd started making our fancy-dress costumes instead.

"Oh, that's great, Kenny!" Rosie said as she unwrapped the scented bath stuff I'd bought her. She'd already got a box of choccies from Frankie, a set of different nail varnishes from Fliss and a groovy pink fluffy purse, shaped like a heart, from Lyndz.

"Now you won't smell like a monkey even if you look like one!" I pointed out, and Rosie thumped me.

"Hey, take a look over there," Frankie said suddenly in a low voice.

We all glanced across the playground. Pilar, Isabella and the others were standing in the corner chatting away to – you've guessed it, the Gruesome Twosome themselves, the M&Ms.

"They're getting pretty matey, aren't they?" Lyndz said.

"Not for long!" I said confidently. "You wait till we get into class and I show them Mrs Weaver's computer list!"

We all started grinning and giving each other high fives. Pilar and the others were going to find out exactly what the M&Ms were really like!

"I guess we can't blame the Spanish girls for being mad about those emails," Lyndz said as we charged into school the minute the bell rang. "I mean, they must have thought we were being really nasty."

"Yeah, well, they should have known we'd never do anything like that!" I retorted. "And they could have asked us about them first instead of getting their knickers all in a twist!"

"What, you mean, like you'd have done if someone had sent you nasty emails?" Lyndz said with a grin.

"Oh, yeah, right!" Fliss chimed in sarcastically. "As if Kenny wouldn't have flattened them first and asked questions later!"

"All right, all right!" I groaned. "Let's just get this sorted, OK?" I slung my tracky top on to my coat peg and headed for the classroom, the others right behind me. We'd rushed into school so fast that we were first through the door. We had to get our hands on that computer list before the M&Ms arrived and realised what we were up to!

The classroom noticeboard was behind Mrs Weaver's table, next to the board. It was usually full of notices about the football and netball teams, the various school clubs and lots of other stuff, including the computer rota. *Usually*…

"Girls! One at a time, please!" Mrs Weaver snapped as we all tried to elbow our way through the door at the same time. She was standing by her table, sorting through a pile of folders. "I know it's getting towards the end of term, but there's no need to behave like a bunch of football hooligans!"

"Yes Miss, sorry Miss," we all said together.

Then I stopped dead and nudged Frankie hard in the ribs. She nudged Fliss and Fliss nudged Lyndz and Lyndz did the same to Rosie. We all stared at the noticeboard on the wall. The *empty* noticeboard.

There wasn't a single piece of paper pinned up on it at all. Everything had vanished – including the computer list!

"Miss, what happened to the stuff that was on the noticeboard?" I gabbled.

It was then that I noticed the two large, bulging black bags lying next to Mrs Weaver's table.

"Oh, I've thrown all that away now," Mrs Weaver replied, ripping up a couple of sheets of paper and shoving them into one of the bin bags. "The whole classroom's got to be cleared by the end of term, so I'll be needing some help this week." She raised her eyebrows at us. "Any volunteers?"

We were too busy staring at each other in horror to reply. The computer list was now in one of those two bulging black bags! How were we going to get it back?

"Um – the thing is, Miss," I said, "there was something on the noticeboard I really needed. Can I go through the bags and look for it?"

Mrs Weaver stared at me as if I'd gone mad. "Don't be ridiculous, Laura! You'll never find it – in fact, it's probably been ripped into pieces!"

I just couldn't believe it. That list had been our one chance of proving to Maria and the others that we hadn't sent those emails. Now we didn't have a hope!

"But, Miss—" I began.

"Leave it, Kenny." Frankie grabbed my arm and pulled me away as the rest of the class began to come in. "There's nothing we can do about it!"

"Rats!" I muttered under my breath as Mrs Weaver picked up the bags and went out to throw them into the huge steel bins behind the canteen. "What about if I climb into the bins at lunch time and try to find it then?"

"Urgh, don't be so disgusting!" Fliss wrinkled up her nose. "Anyway, Mrs Poole said anyone who climbs into those bins is going to be in big trouble."

"Yeah, that was just because Ryan Scott did it last year for a dare and got stuck!" I retorted. "But that wouldn't happen to me."

"Forget it, Kenny!" Frankie said firmly. "You wouldn't know which bin it was – you wouldn't even know which *bag* it was. It'd take forever!"

"We can't just give up!" I muttered as Isabella, Maria, Pilar, Elena and Anna came in, talking and laughing with the M&Ms. What was worse, they even went over to sit on their table with them!

"Hurry up and settle down," Mrs Weaver called, as the rest of the Spanish kids came in with Miss Moreno and Mr Cortez. "We've got a visitor arriving in a moment or two – a photographer from the local newspaper!"

We all looked at each other in surprise.

"The paper has heard about our visitors from Spain, and it wants to do a piece about them," Mrs Weaver went on. "So we're all going to have our photo taken, and hopefully it will be in the newspaper tonight!"

Everyone started talking at once, while Mrs Weaver went over to speak to the two Spanish teachers.

"We're going to be in the paper!" Fliss squealed. "Quick, where's my comb?"

"Cool!" said Rosie. "Let's make sure we get to the front!"

"Yeah, we will!" I said in a determined voice, "Even if we have to trample all over the M&Ms to do it!"

"Look!" Frankie whispered, elbowing me in the ribs. "Maria's coming over!"

Pretty shocked, we all stopped talking. But Maria was actually *smiling*. Well, sort of.

"Hi." Maria stopped in front of us, looking a bit shy. "I come to say – we are sorry about the makeover."

That was a *big* shock! Our mouths dropped open and none of us could say a word for a second or two.

"That's OK," Frankie said at last.

"And I'm sorry about breaking Isabella's present for her mum," Fliss chimed in quickly.

Maria shrugged. "It was accident, no? So, we are friends again?"

The Sleepover Club all looked at each other.

"What about the M&Ms?" I asked.

"Who?" Maria looked blank.

"Emma and Emily," Rosie explained.

"Oh, we can *all* be friends, can't we?" Maria asked.

"Not on your flippin' life!" I began until both Frankie and Lyndz trod heavily on my toes under the table. "Ow!"

"Great!" Maria put her hand in her pocket, and popped a sweet into her mouth. "Sorry, you want one?" She pulled out a bag of liquorice and held it out to us.

"We're not supposed to eat in class," Fliss began virtuously, but Frankie gave her a look.

"Come on, Fliss, it's the end of term! Take a risk!"

We all took a sweet from Maria and quickly popped them in our mouths before Mrs Weaver saw us. It looked like we'd managed to sort things out with the Spanish girls after all! Although there was no way we were going to be friends with the M&Ms...

"We see you at playtime, yes?" Maria winked at us and went back to the others, just as a man with a camera hanging round his neck popped his head round the door.

"Mrs Weaver? I'm James Robinson from the *Evening Echo*."

"Oh, good, come in." Mrs Weaver ushered him in, while Fliss grabbed her comb and started preening herself. "Now, what would you like us to do?"

"Well, if we could gather everyone at the front of the room, with the Spanish children in the middle, that would make it easier for me to get everyone into the picture," the photographer said.

We spent the next few minutes pushing

tables and chairs around, and being posed by the photographer.

"There's no way I'm being best buddies with the M&Ms!" I muttered to Frankie as we carried a table between us. "Not even to make friends with Maria and the others again!"

"Let's just wait and see what happens, OK?" Frankie replied in a low voice, still chewing on her sweet.

Finally, everything was ready. We hadn't quite managed to get to the front of the photo because the photographer wanted the Spanish kids there, but we were right behind them, kneeling on a couple of tables, with the rest of our class around us.

"Right, now let's have some nice big smiles please!" called Mr Robinson.

We all began to smile – and then we all nearly jumped out of our skins as Mrs Weaver gave a loud scream.

"Laura! Francesca! Lyndsey! Felicity! Rosie! What on *earth* has happened to your teeth? They're all *black!*"

CHAPTER SEVEN

"What?" I said, puzzled. I didn't have a clue what Mrs Weaver was going on about – until I glanced at Frankie. It looked like she had no teeth at all because they were totally black! And the rest of the Sleepover Club were just the same!

"You've obviously been eating something you shouldn't have!" Mrs Weaver said grimly. "I suggest you go and wash your mouths out!"

"But, Mrs Weaver, we'll miss the photo!" Fliss gasped.

"That's OK, girls," said the photographer with a grin. "You'll only frighten the readers looking like that, anyway!"

Everyone started laughing, especially the Spanish girls and the M&Ms, who were just about killing themselves. Angrily the five of us stomped out of the classroom, and went into the girls' toilets.

"We've missed our chance to be in the newspaper because of that trick Maria played on us!" Fliss said crossly as she rinsed her mouth out. "Those were joke sweets!"

"I thought they tasted a bit funny!" Lyndz said as she used her finger as a toothbrush.

"I guess that was to pay us back for breaking Isabella's bowl," I muttered. "They must have thought we did it on purpose."

"And I bet the M&Ms have been egging them on as well!" Frankie added. "You know what those two are like!"

"Yeah, well, we're not going to let them get away with it, are we?" I asked. "This means WAR!"

The others looked at each other and nodded, although they all looked a bit glum. It *was* a bit of a downer after we'd looked forward to the Spanish girls visiting for so long, but we couldn't let the M&Ms walk all over us, could we?

By the time we got back to the classroom, the photographer had gone and the rest of the class were moving all the chairs and tables back into place.

"Oh, there you are," said Mrs Weaver sternly as she stared at us. "I suppose that was meant to be funny! Well, if you girls have any more jokes like that lined up, you won't be taking part in any of the end-of-term activities. Do I make myself clear?"

"Yes, Miss," we mumbled together, trying not to look at the Spanish girls and the M&Ms, who were all grinning.

While we were putting our table and chairs back in place, the M&Ms came over to have a quick gloat.

"I don't think Mrs Weaver's too pleased with you!" Emma Hughes said gleefully. "And *what* a shame you aren't going to get your picture in the paper!"

"Our friends the Spanish girls are really fed

up with you!" Emily Berryman chimed in smugly. "They wish they were staying with us instead of with you lot!"

"Oh, take a jump off a very high cliff, you two!" I snapped.

The M&Ms went off, giggling. They went back over to Pilar and the others, and they all put their heads together and started whispering and sniggering.

"You know what?" I said to the others as we all sat down. "I'm going to think up a really gruesome trick to play on that lot on the last day of term!"

"No way, Kenny!" Fliss said firmly. "You know what Mrs Poole said about playing tricks at the end of term – she banned them!"

"Yeah, that was after some of the leavers flour-bombed her in the corridor!" Frankie giggled.

"Hey, I wish I'd seen that!" Rosie said.

"It was before you started here," Lyndz said. "*And* they threw eggs at the teachers' cars – it was really funny!"

"Quiet, please." Mrs Weaver was looking

round the room waiting for everyone to settle down. "Right, we have a couple of things to sort out. As you know, it's Sports Day tomorrow and then it's the school Summer Fair the day after."

That cheered us up a bit. Sports Day was a great laugh. We'd held the heats a few days before Pilar and the rest of her gang had arrived, and all of us had made it into at least one of the races which would be taking place tomorrow, even Fliss.

"Right, don't forget that those of you who are taking part in the races tomorrow must have your sports kit with you," Mrs Weaver went on, "or you won't be allowed to compete. Do ask your mums and dads to come along if they can. And, by the way, I'm sure you'll be pleased to know that our visitors will be taking part in the races too!"

We all sat up when we heard *that!* Well, I was going to make sure that if Maria or the others were in any of the races *I* was in, I was going to beat the pants off them!

"And now for the Summer Fair on

Wednesday afternoon," Mrs Weaver went on. "As you know, it's organised by some of the parents…"

We all started nudging Lyndz, because her mum, Mrs Collins, was in charge of the Parents' Association.

"… and this year it's our class's turn to help out." Mrs Weaver glanced round the room. "Everyone, including our visitors, will be given a job to do, and please try to do it *sensibly*. You'll have plenty of time to have a look at the stalls and enjoy yourselves, but the parents who are organising the fair are relying on your help as well."

"I hope we get to do something good!" I whispered to Frankie.

Mrs Weaver glanced at the list she was holding. Then she frowned and glanced at us. "Francesca, Laura, Felicity, Lyndsey and Rosie – Mrs Collins has suggested that you be in charge of the tombola."

"Excellent!" I muttered to Frankie.

"I just hope I can trust you to behave yourselves," Mrs Weaver said sternly, fixing us with her beadiest stare. "You know that the Mayoress is coming to open the fair, and we don't want anything going wrong."

"No, Miss," we said virtuously. The tombola was one of the best stalls to be on, so we were all pretty excited. We were even more pleased when the M&Ms got the boring job of selling programmes, and Pilar and the others were put down to help Lyndz's mum with the cake stall! That was one in the eye for them!

"And don't forget that we have our class trip to the theme park next Monday." Mrs Weaver had to raise her voice because the bell had gone for break time and everyone was talking again. "Plus the fancy-dress competition on the last day of term. I hope you're all busy making your costumes!"

"Oh, yes, Miss!" said Emma Hughes in a treacly voice. "I'm working really hard on mine!"

"So am I, Miss!" said Emily Berryman.

"We can't let those creeps win *again*!" I said, as we went outside. "They've walked off with the prizes the last three times!"

"Still, we got the best job at the Summer

Fair!" said Lyndz. "I had to nag my mum for ages to give us the tombola!"

"Nice one!" I said, as we all crowded round Lyndz and slapped her on the back. "Hey, maybe we can fix it so we win all the prizes!"

"What about Sports Day tomorrow?" Rosie asked. She hadn't been to Sports Day at our school before. "Do you get a prize if you win?"

"Yeah, book tokens usually," said Frankie.

"Let's see how many the Sleepover Club can win!" I said.

"I tell you – none at all!" Maria said scornfully. We hadn't heard the Spanish girls come up behind us, and now they were giggling and sticking their tongues out at us.

"We'll win every race we're in!" I snapped. "Just wait and see!"

Fliss looked a bit nervous at that. She'd made it into the skipping race, but only because Ryan Scott had tripped over his rope and knocked over three other kids, including Frankie, in their heat.

"*We* win more than you!" Pilar retorted. "We are better at sport!"

"No way!" Frankie cut in.

"Then we have competition, yes?" said Maria. "We see who wins the most prizes. If you win – we give you all our prizes. If *we* get more, you give us *your* prizes!"

"OK – but this is just between us, not the M&Ms as well!" I said firmly. Maria nodded, and I stuck out my hand, and we shook. She tried to crush my fingers but I was ready for her, and I crushed hers instead! "You're on!"

CHAPTER EIGHT

"I wish we weren't having this stupid contest!" Fliss moaned for about the millionth time as we changed into our sports kit the following afternoon. Sports Day was due to start in the next half hour, and we were all up for it! At least, I thought we were...

"Stop saying that, will you!" I poked her in the back. "We've got to win, so I hope you've been practising your skipping!"

Fliss didn't look too happy. "Well, sort of..." she muttered. "But Pilar's in the skipping race too, and Isabella says Pilar's really good at skipping so—"

"Hang on a minute!" I grabbed Fliss's arm. "*What* did you say?"

Fliss turned bright red. "Nothing."

"You said *Isabella* told you!" I stared hard at Fliss. "Have you been talking to her?"

"No. Well. Yes. A bit." Fliss looked even more flustered.

"I don't believe you, you traitor!" I snapped. "What're you talking to our enemies for?"

"Well, she's sharing my bedroom, and we just got talking last night," Fliss defended herself. "I think she wants to be friends with us again!"

"I bet it's some sort of con!" I said crossly. "And you fell for it, Fliss! You're such a wally!"

"I am not!" Fliss snapped.

"Yeah? Well, you're the *only* one of us who wants to make friends with them after what they did!" And I looked round at the others.

Lyndz had gone a bit pink, and was clearing her throat and shuffling her feet.

"Um – me and Elena sort of got talking last night too," she confessed.

"What!" I glared at her. "What did she say?"

"She said she wished we were all friends again," Lyndz muttered, "But that Maria and some of the others were still mad at us."

"There you are then!" I said triumphantly, as Mrs Weaver began to round everyone up to take us over to the sports field. "They don't like us and we don't like them!"

Lyndz and Fliss looked doubtful, and so did Frankie and Rosie! I was really beginning to lose my cool now.

"Well, if Isabella and Elena want to be friends," Frankie said slowly, "maybe we should all give it a go—"

"No way!" I cut in firmly. "Look what they did to us – they can't get away with that!" Secretly I was a bit annoyed that Maria hadn't said she wanted to make friends with *me* again. We'd got on really well in Spain… But if she was going to be mean, then so was I – and I could be a lot meaner than she could! "Anyway," I went on, "we don't want to be mates with them while they're hanging round with the M&Ms, do we?"

The others shook their heads, although

Lyndz and Fliss still looked a bit uncertain.

"Come on, line up in twos, please," Mrs Weaver called. "When we get to the field, I want you sitting in rows ready for your races, just like we practised last week."

We all lined up by the classroom door. Rosie went over to get something from her locker – and I couldn't believe my eyes when I saw Anna go over to talk to her! They were smiling at each other too! So when Rosie came back to line up, I pounced on her straightaway.

"What did Anna say to you?"

"Er – she just wished me good luck," Rosie muttered, looking embarrassed.

"Oh, don't tell me – you and Anna are big buddies again!" I said sarcastically. I was pleased to see that it looked like Maria was telling Anna off for speaking to Rosie too! At this rate, there wouldn't be any contest if everyone started being mates again... Deep down I wasn't sure if I was glad or sorry. But if Maria wasn't giving in, then neither was I!

The rest of the school was already out on the field by the time our class got there. There were lots of parents there too, sitting on chairs next to the track so that they got a good view. There was a refreshments stall, and a little platform where Mrs Poole stood to present the prizes at the end.

"There's my mum!" Fliss started waving madly at Mrs Sidebotham, who was sitting next to Mrs Thomas, Frankie's mum. Mrs Thomas was a few months pregnant, and a bump was beginning to show.

"Save your energy for the skipping race, Fliss!" I told her.

The first race for our year was the girls' sprint. I was in that, and so was Frankie. So were Maria and Pilar! I nudged Frankie as they lined up next to us.

"Go for it, Franks!" I whispered. Frankie was faster than me, and I reckoned she could easily beat Pilar and Maria too! But if I could get second place, I'd win a prize too. That would put us ahead in the contest right from the start!

"You have no chance!" Maria said as we waited for Mrs Weaver to blow her whistle.

"We beat the trousers off you!"

"You mean beat the pants off us!" I corrected her. "And you won't, so dream on!"

"On your marks!" Mrs Weaver shouted. "Get set!" And then she blew the whistle. Frankie shot off like a bullet from a gun, and she was halfway down the track before I'd even moved. I ran as fast as I could, but Pilar overtook me easily, although she couldn't catch Frankie. I could hear Fliss, Rosie and Lyndz cheering me on, and I tried even harder, but I couldn't overtake Pilar. Then I heard footsteps behind me – Maria was catching me up!

I had to really push it to stay ahead of her. Frankie got to the tape first, followed by Pilar and I was third – with Maria about a millimetre behind me! Panting hard, I slapped Frankie on the back.

"Nice one! We got two prizes – that means we're in the lead!"

"You were lucky!" Maria snapped. "We beat you in the next race!" And she stormed off.

"Well done, Frankie," Pilar said quickly,

before she ran off after Maria.

Frankie looked surprised. "That was nice of her," she said.

"Don't *you* go all soft on me!" I said crossly, giving her a shove.

There were some other races next, involving some of the other kids, so we sat and watched. Then it was time for our year again. It was the sack race, and Rosie and Isabella were taking part in it.

"Watch out for Ryan Scott, Rosie-Posie!" I told her as Rosie lined up inside her sack. It was a mixed race so there were boys and girls in it together. "He's pretty fast."

"Yeah, he can jump like a frog!" Frankie added with a grin.

"He looks like one too!" I said under my breath, and we all giggled.

"Hey, I heard that!" Ryan shouted, poking me in the back.

"On your marks!" Mrs Weaver called.

"I wonder if Isabella's any good at sack racing?" Lyndz said as we waited for the whistle to blow.

"She's got no chance against Rosie!" I said confidently.

The race began. We were all yelling and cheering loudly for Rosie, but although she was jumping along so fast she was purple in the face, we could see that she wasn't going to win. Ryan Scott was leaping along in front of everyone else, and he was miles ahead. Emma Hughes was second, and Danny McCloud was third, close behind her!

I groaned. "We haven't got a chance of winning a prize!"

"Well, neither has Isabella!" Frankie pointed out. Isabella was ahead of Rosie, but she was only in fourth place.

Then, all of a sudden, Ryan Scott tried to jump too far. He fell forward and landed flat on his face! Emma Hughes began grinning, thinking that she was going to win, when next second Danny McCloud stumbled, fell over and knocked the Queen over too! We all started cheering – but then I stopped. Isabella was in the lead now and she was jumping neatly towards the finishing-line!

"Come on, Rosie!" I yelled, but it was too late. Isabella had won! And Rosie was last – that meant we were equal with two prizes each...

Maria tapped me on the shoulder. "We catch you up – and now we beat you!" she said with a big grin.

"We'll see!" I retorted, as Rosie trailed over to us, looking a bit sheepish.

"Sorry," she muttered.

"Oh, it doesn't matter," Lyndz told her.

"What d'you mean? Of *course* it matters!" I yelled. "We've got to beat Maria and that lot out of sight! And that means you've all got to try harder!"

The others didn't look that keen, and that made me mad. Just because *they* were all being wimps and wanting to be friends with the Spanish girls again – well, *I* wasn't! Although I might have given in if Maria had been a bit nicer... But she was too busy shouting at the other girls in Spanish – probably telling *them* they had to try harder too!

Anyway, we had some ups and some downs during the next few races. Lyndz and Frankie won the three-legged race which put us ahead, but then Anna evened things up by winning the obstacle race. Maria and Elena came second and third in the Potato Grab, but then Frankie won the egg and spoon and I was second in the hurdles. So by the time we got to the last race, the skipping race, we were on a dead heat with five prizes each.

"You'd better win this, Fliss!" I said in a determined voice.

Fliss looked a bit pale. "I'm not very good at skipping," she muttered.

"You're going to win this race if it kills you!" I told her.

"I feel sick!" Fliss moaned. "I don't want to do it!"

"Hey, that's an idea!" I bounced to my feet. "Fliss, go and tell Mrs W. you feel ill, and you don't want to be in the race. Then Frankie can take your place – she's the best skipper out of all of us! And she would have been in the race anyway if Ryan Scott hadn't knocked her over in the heats."

"Do I have to?" Frankie grumbled, looking less than keen.

"Yeah, you do!" I said firmly. What was going on here? Looked like I was trying to run this feud single-handed, because the others just didn't seem interested...

Looking relieved, Fliss went off to speak to Mrs Weaver. Meanwhile I glanced over at Maria and the others. Maria was having a real go at Pilar in Spanish, waving her arms about and talking really loudly. I guessed that Maria was saying that Pilar had to win the race – but Pilar looked about as keen as Frankie did.

"OK, it's all sorted." Fliss came back. "Frankie's in."

"Oh, great," Frankie muttered.

They all lined up for the skipping race. Maria looked well sick when she saw that Frankie had taken Fliss's place, and she came storming over to me.

"Where is Fliss? She should be in this race!"

"Fliss isn't very well," I said coolly, "so Frankie's doing it instead."

"You make that up!" Maria snapped. "You know Fliss will not beat Pilar!"

"Prove it!" I retorted, glaring at her until Elena and Anna came over and dragged her away.

"On your marks!" called Mrs Weaver. "Get set!"

The whistle blew.

"Go for it, Frankie!" I yelled.

Pilar and Frankie sped off neck and neck. They both had long legs so they could take big strides, and they'd soon left the others behind. But they were still so close together, it was hard to tell which one of them was in the lead. First it looked like it was Frankie, then Pilar.

"COME ON, FRANKIE!" I shouted.

And then it happened. Pilar's skipping rope suddenly hooked itself on to one of the gold earrings she was wearing. She skidded to a halt and gave a yell, trying desperately to untangle it.

"Go, Frankie!" I leapt to my feet gleefully. We had the race in the bag now!

Then I just couldn't believe my eyes. Frankie stopped skipping and dashed over to Pilar! She started trying to help her untangle the rope, but it was well and truly stuck. A few seconds later, everyone else in the race skipped past them!

"Frankie!" I screamed, dancing up and down in frustration. "Go on! Don't stop!"

But it was too late. Everyone else had already crossed the finishing-line!

CHAPTER NINE

"All right, Kenny, stop going on about it, will you!" Frankie snapped as she threw a handful of raffle tickets into the tombola drum. "It was no big deal!"

"No big deal!" I retorted. "You stopped to help Pilar, which meant we didn't win the race! We could have walked it – *and* we'd have got their book tokens too!"

"Frankie was just trying to help Pilar," Lyndz chimed in.

"Yeah, her ear was all red and sore afterwards, didn't you see?" Rosie added.

"I think it was really nice of Frankie to stop

and help," Fliss said.

It was the day after Sports Day, and it was almost time for the Summer Fair to start. All the stalls had been set up on the sports field that morning, and there was a long queue of people at the gates, waiting to come in. We'd all really been looking forward to the fair, but after yesterday we weren't getting on too well. We didn't argue very often, but now the others were really bugging me. I knew they all wanted to get matey with the Spanish girls again, but there was *no way* I was up for that! Not while Maria was still keeping the war between us going.

Maria and the others were over on the cake stall with Lyndz's mum, and they were all looking pretty sulky. I reckoned Maria was having exactly the same problem as me...

"If you and Maria would just sort things out, we could all be mates again!" Frankie said, throwing some more tickets into the drum.

"Well, she started it!" I retorted.

"You two are as bad as each other!" Frankie said. "You both need a kick up the behind!"

"Maria's a pain!" I said crossly. "I wish Molly the Monster was back home instead of her!"

"Well, you'd better behave yourself today," Fliss warned me, as Mrs Weaver walked round inspecting the stalls. "Mrs Weaver's got her beady eye on you!"

"We've got some good prizes, haven't we?" Lyndz looked at our stall. We had a mixture of cuddly toys, bath stuff, sweets and bottles of soft drink. "I *love* this Dalmatian!"

The stuffed Dalmatian was our best prize, and Frankie had sat him right at the front of the stall where everyone could see him. He was really big and made of soft white fur. I wasn't into cuddly toys much, but even I wouldn't have minded winning him! All the winning tickets ended in 0 or 5, and the Dalmatian was number 500.

"That should get a lot of people coming to our stall!" Frankie said.

"Hey, I've just had an idea!" I announced. "Why don't we challenge Maria and that lot to see which of us makes more money on our stall?"

The others groaned. "No, Kenny!" they said together.

"Oh, well, if you want to be a bunch of wimps..." I muttered.

"Look, the caretaker's opening the gates," Lyndz said quickly. "And here comes Mrs Poole with the Mayoress!"

All the people queuing outside started to file in. They crowded round the little platform, which had been left there yesterday after Sports Day. Mrs Pontefract, the Mayoress, was chatting to Mrs Poole as she went up on to the platform to make a speech. Mrs Weaver had warned us that we weren't allowed to sell a single ticket until she'd declared the fair open.

"Well, firstly let me say how very happy I am to be here," declared Mrs Pontefract, looking at all the people clustered round the platform. She was wearing her robes and gold chain, but because she was very short and round, she looked like a Teletubby! Mrs Pontefract had been to our school a few times before, and whenever she made a speech she always went on and on, so none of us bothered listening.

"I wonder who'll win the Dalmatian," said Fliss, giving it a pat.

"I bet it's still left over at the end," I said. "The best prizes always are!"

"... and now I am happy to declare this Summer Fair open!" said the Mayoress, and everyone clapped. Then they all started rushing over to the stalls. Mrs Poole and Mrs Pontefract left the platform, and they started looking round the fair too.

"Hello, I want to buy some tickets," said a familiar voice. We all looked round, and there was Isabella with her purse in her hand.

"That was quick!" said Fliss with a shy smile. "You're our first customer, Isabella!"

"Hold on – you're supposed to be helping Lyndz's mum on the cake stall, aren't you?" I asked, glaring at Isabella.

"Mrs Collins say I can come and buy some tickets." Isabella pointed at the Dalmatian. "I want to win this!"

"Yeah, he's gorgeous, isn't he?" Frankie said enthusiastically.

Isabella held out a pound coin. "Please can

I have five tickets?"

"I suppose so," I muttered, taking the money.

"Isabella!" Maria slipped out from behind the cake stall and rushed over to her. She gave me an evil stare, and then began jabbering away in Spanish to Isabella. Even though we couldn't understand what they were saying, it was obvious they were having an argument. I guessed that Maria didn't want Isabella to buy any tickets from us!

Isabella wouldn't take any notice though. She put her hand into the drum, and pulled out some folded tickets. She took three herself and gave two of them to Maria to open.

"Anything ending in 0 or 5 wins a prize!" Lyndz said helpfully, and I glanced at her, annoyed. I didn't want Isabella to win *anything*!

Isabella said something in Spanish and threw her tickets in the bin by the side of the stall, looking disappointed. Meanwhile, Maria was looking at one of the two tickets she had in her hand with a big smile on her face.

"I win a prize!" She grinned smugly at me. "I

have a number with 0 at the end!"

"Trust her!" I muttered to Frankie.

"I have number 500!" Maria announced, waving the ticket over her head.

"Yes! We win the dog!" Isabella shouted, beaming all over her face.

"No, you can't have!" I gasped, and the other Sleepovers looked gobsmacked too. Our best prize *couldn't* have been won by the first customer who bought a ticket! And there was no way I was letting Maria and Isabella have it!

"Yes! We win!" Maria and Isabella were celebrating, doing high fives, but I had an idea. Quickly I whipped the 500 ticket off the front of the Dalmatian and swopped it with the one on a can of Coca Cola, which had 225 on it. The other Sleepovers could hardly believe their eyes!

"Kenny, you can't do that!" Fliss began, but I elbowed her in the ribs. "Ow!"

"Here's your prize, Isabella," I said casually. "A can of Coke!"

Maria and Isabella stared at me. "No, I win the dog!" Isabella said with a frown.

"No, I don't think so!" I shook my head. "The Dalmatian's number 225!"

Isabella and Maria both blinked as if they were seeing things. "No, it was 500!" Isabella said furiously. "You change it so we do not win!"

"I did not!" I said.

"You should let us have a free go!" Maria said, trying to grab some more tickets out of the tombola drum.

"No way!" I legged it round to the front of the stall, and tried to push her away, but Maria picked the drum up off the stall and held it tightly.

"Give it back!" I yelled, and we started to have a tug-of-war!

By now quite a lot of people were looking round at us to see what was going on. I was so mad I didn't care, not even when I saw that Mrs Poole and the Mayoress were heading in our direction. Pilar and the other Spanish girls also dashed over from the cake stall to find out what was happening, and they started calling to Maria in Spanish.

"Kenny, stop it!" Frankie was saying, and so were the others, but I just pulled my end of the tombola drum even harder.

Unfortunately, the drum was a bit rickety and it couldn't take the strain. It split in two, and Maria and I both fell backwards...

"What on earth's going on here?" Mrs Poole began with a frown, but next second she and the Mayoress were both showered in *hundreds* of raffle tickets!

CHAPTER TEN

"Well?"

Mrs Poole sat at her desk the following morning and stared hard at the ten of us lined up in a row – me and the rest of the Sleepover Club as well as Maria and the Spanish girls. Usually Mrs P. was a bit of a pushover, and talked more about how sorry she was that we'd let her down, rather than just going ballistic. But this time she looked like she was going to tear us to bits.

"I was very ashamed of your behaviour in front of all our visitors, *and* the Mayoress too," Mrs Poole went on sternly. "Poor Mrs Pontefract was picking raffle tickets out of her hat for at least ten minutes afterwards."

I bit my lip, hoping I looked upset, but really I was trying not to laugh! We'd spent the rest of the Summer Fair on our hands and knees sweeping up the tombola tickets, and we'd had tellings-off from Mrs Weaver, the Mayoress and from Lyndz's mum. Now it was Mrs Poole's turn.

"There'd better be a good reason for such appalling behaviour," Mrs Poole went on, looking hard at us, one by one, "or I'm afraid to say that none of you will be going on the class trip to the theme park next Monday."

That wiped the smile off my face! I'd been looking forward to going to WonderLand for months, and now it was all Maria's fault that I might not be going. Well, I suppose it was my fault a bit as well... Anyway, I knew I'd have to speak up and tell the truth, because I couldn't let the others take the blame when they'd had nothing to do with it. So I cleared my throat.

"Er – Mrs Poole, I—"

"Mrs Poole, I tell you what happened," Isabella interrupted me, and I glared at her. I reckoned Isabella was now going to drop me right in it by telling Mrs Poole all about how she'd won the Dalmatian and I'd switched the tickets round!

"I buy some tickets," Isabella said in a loud voice. "I ask Maria to help me pull them out and she have her hand stuck in the tombola."

Mrs Poole frowned. "So why were she and Kenny fighting over it?"

What's going on? I wondered with a frown. Why wasn't Isabella dropping me in it? I just couldn't understand it.

"They weren't fighting, Mrs Poole," Frankie said quickly. "Kenny was just trying to pull Maria's hand free."

"Yes, and the tombola break," Pilar added.

"And that's when all the tickets flew out," Lyndz finished off.

"We're really sorry, Mrs Poole," said Rosie.

Mrs Poole looked slightly less furious. "Is that what happened, Maria? Kenny?"

I glanced sideways at Maria. She looked pretty sulky, but Pilar was nudging her in the ribs.

"Yes, Mrs Poole," she muttered.

"Yes, Mrs Poole," I said, heaving a silent sigh of relief. It looked like I wasn't going to be banned from the trip after all, but I just couldn't understand why. Maria had had the perfect opportunity to get me into trouble big-time and she hadn't taken it. Why not? Now that Isabella had helped me out too, I felt really bad that she'd hadn't got the Dalmatian in the end. Maria had dropped the winning ticket in all the fuss after the tombola had broken.

"Well, if it was an accident, I think I can overlook it just this once," said Mrs Poole. "But I want you all to spend this morning writing letters of apology to Mrs Pontefract. And I want them given to me by the end of the morning. Is that clear?"

We all nodded. We'd got off pretty lightly, considering we'd annoyed the Mayoress *and* the headteacher! And at least we were all still going on the class trip. We all filed out of Mrs Poole's office trying not to grin at each other with relief.

"Whew, that was close!" I said to Frankie as

soon as we were outside in the corridor. "I thought I was going to miss out on WonderLand!"

"Well, you were lucky Isabella thought fast and came up with a good excuse!" Frankie told me. "You owe her one!"

"Yeah, OK…" I muttered. Then I noticed the other Sleepovers staring hard at me. "What?"

"Isabella got you out of trouble," said Fliss pointedly. "You *could* say thank you!"

I pulled a face. "Oh, all right then…"

"And maybe you and Maria can make friends now," Lyndz added eagerly.

I didn't say anything. I was beginning to feel a bit ashamed of myself for messing about with the tickets the day before. Maybe if I asked Mrs Poole nicely she'd let Isabella have the Dalmatian after all…

The Spanish girls were crowded round Maria, who still looked sulky, and they were having a go at her in Spanish. I reckoned they were telling her to make up with me. If she wanted to, well, so would I.

"Er – Isabella, thanks for coming up with

that story for Mrs Poole," I muttered. "It was really nice of you."

Isabella grinned at me. "It is OK!"

"And I'm really sorry about changing the ticket on the Dalmatian," I went on. "I'll tell Mrs Poole you won it fair and square, and maybe she'll let you have it."

For some reason Isabella stopped smiling and looked over at Maria. "Do you tell her or do I?" she asked sternly.

"Tell me what?" I asked, puzzled.

Maria was staring down at her feet. "I did not have the winning ticket," she muttered sheepishly.

"*What?*" My mouth fell open. "But you had number 500!"

"No, it was not 500," Maria said. "I just *say* I had it to make you angry! I knew you do not want to give Isabella your best prize!"

"What a stupid trick to pull!" I was so furious I could hardly speak. "I nearly lost out on the class trip because of you!"

"Well, you should not change the tickets!" Maria snapped.

"I wouldn't have had to if you hadn't told that fib in the first place!" I retorted.

"Oh, you're both as bad as each other!" Frankie cut in. "Why don't you just give it up and make friends?"

"Yes, and then we forget all about this!" Pilar added.

"I'll be friends with Pilar, Elena, Anna and Isabella," I said pointedly, "but I'm not going to be friends with *her*!"

"And I am friends with Frankie, Fliss, Rosie and Lyndz," Maria said, "but I am not friends with *her*!"

"Fine!" I snapped.

"Fine!" agreed Maria.

And we turned on our heels and stalked off in opposite directions, leaving the others behind us.

CHAPTER ELEVEN

"WonderLand, here we come!" I said as I climbed on to the coach behind Fliss. "This is going to be cool!"

We'd just had another weekend without a sleepover because of the Oldies still making a fuss about the food fight, so this trip to WonderLand would make up for that.

"We only just made it, though!" Frankie pointed out.

"Yeah, so don't do anything crazy today, Kenny!" Fliss warned me.

"Me! Why should *I* be the one to do anything crazy?" I asked innocently, poking Fliss hard in the back. She squealed and nearly whacked Emma Hughes on the head with her rucksack as she went past her seat.

"Watch where you're going, you idiot!" Emma snorted.

"Yeah," chimed in Emily Berryman, who was sitting next to her. "You could have taken Emma's head off!"

"That would have been an improvement!" I said sweetly, and the Terrible Twins both glared at me.

Maria and Pilar were sitting behind the M&Ms, with Elena and Anna behind them, and Isabella was across the aisle on her own. Anyway, when I made that crack about Emma, I *thought* I saw Maria *almost* smile. But maybe I didn't really. Maybe I imagined it... After all, we still weren't speaking to each other, and the others had given up trying to make us. They couldn't really be friends properly unless me and Maria were too, so the Spanish girls were still going round with the M&Ms.

We all went further on down the coach, and sat down – me next to Lyndz, Fliss next to

Rosie and Frankie on her own.

"What have you got in your packed lunch?" Lyndz asked as soon as we sat down.

"Two packets of cheese and onion crisps, two ham and tomato rolls, a Snickers, a Twix, a packet of chocolate Hob-Nobs and a strawberry milkshake," I said.

"I'll swop you a packet of salt and vinegar for a cheese and onion," Lyndz offered.

"And I'll swop a sausage roll for half your Hob-Nobs," Fliss said.

Anyway, swopping and changing our lunchboxes around took up lots of time, and by the time we arrived at WonderLand, we all had totally different lunches from the ones we'd set out with! Then we all stopped thinking about food for once, and started getting pretty excited instead. Fliss had been to WonderLand before, but none of the rest of us had. It looked pretty spectacular. The front was built like a huge castle, and you had to walk on a drawbridge over a moat to get in.

"Wow! This is coo-ell!" I gasped as the coach pulled up in the car park next to all the others.

"What's the best ride, Flissy?"

"I liked the riverboat ride," Fliss said.

"Oh, great big fat hairy deal!" I snorted. "I mean, what's the *scariest* ride?"

"The Mega-Loop!" Fliss gave a shudder. "You're upside-down most of the time. I went on it with my mum and my brother, and my mum was sick when we got off!"

"Right, we're definitely going on that one then!" I jumped to my feet. "Come on, what're we waiting for?"

"Sit down, Kenny!" Lyndz grabbed my arm. "Mrs Weaver's waiting to speak to us!"

"Right, I want you all to listen carefully," said Mrs Weaver, who was standing at the front of the coach. "We've talked about this already, but this is a reminder for those of you who don't always act sensibly."

And she stared grimly down the coach at the Sleepover Club. What a cheek!

"You are allowed to go round the theme park on your own, but stay with your friends at all times. Myself and the other teachers will be patrolling around, keeping an eye on things, and if you have any problems, you can always speak to the park stewards."

We were all fidgeting away in our seats with ants in our pants, waiting for Mrs Weaver to stop rabbiting on. As soon as she did, we all jumped up and pushed our way off the coach. Then Mrs W. led us over to one of the ticket offices, and we all got given a luminous pink wristband to wear that would let us go on all the rides.

"Quick, let's get away from the boring old teachers!" I hissed in Frankie's ear as soon as we had gone over the drawbridge and we were inside. Everyone agreed, and we sneaked off while Mrs Weaver was still reminding everyone where we were meeting for lunch, and that we had to be on our best behaviour at all times.

"Come on, let's go on the Secret Garden ride." That was Emma Hughes, wittering on behind us and being a bossy-boots as usual. "It doesn't sound too scary!"

"*That* ride look good." Maria was pointing at a deadly-looking rollercoaster-type ride which towered high above our heads and twisted and turned like a corkscrew.

"That's the Mega-Loop!" Fliss whispered in my ear.

The Queen turned green (hey, I'm a poet!). "No, I don't want to," she said firmly. "Come on!"

I saw Maria pull a face at the others as they trailed off after the M&Ms.

"Poor them!" said Lyndz. "They're going to have a really gruesome time with the M&Ms!"

"Serves Maria right!" I muttered, but secretly I couldn't help feeling a bit sorry for her too. The M&Ms wouldn't want to go on any of the cool rides!

We took it in turns to choose what we wanted to go on. Rosie went first, and she chose the log flume. We all got sore throats because we screamed so much, and we all got soaked, especially me and Frankie 'cos we'd bravely volunteered to sit at the front. But it was a roasting hot day, so we soon dried off!

"Right, my turn now!" Lyndz said when we climbed off. "I want to go on the Jolly Roger!"

That was a huge model of a pirate ship that swung up and down and side to side. It looked fab!

"Look, the queue's pretty small." Frankie nudged me. "Come on!"

We all charged over to join the end of the line. Just as we got there, three older boys we didn't know jumped in and pushed their way in front of us.

"Hey, get out of the way!" I yelled indignantly. "We were here first!"

"No, you weren't!" sniggered one of the boys, who had floppy dark hair and sticking-out ears. "Look, we're in front of you!"

"That's because you pushed in!" Frankie pointed out.

"So make us move then!" said one of the others, a tall skinny boy with ginger hair.

"OK, I will!" I yelled. I charged forward, but I wasn't moving because Fliss and Rosie had both grabbed hold of my arms.

"Kenny, no!" Frankie hissed. "Mrs Weaver"ll go mad if you get into trouble again!"

"Yeah, Kenny! Mrs Weaver'll go mad!"

mocked the third boy, who was short and stocky with a skinhead hair-cut.

If looks could kill, those boys would have dropped down dead! But that was all I could do – look. I didn't want to get into trouble again, and spoil the end of term.

"All right," I muttered, trying to cool myself down. The boys started sniggering and doing high fives because they'd got one over on us, and that *really* made me mad! But I just about managed to stop myself from kicking their butts!

After the Jolly Roger ride, which was really good, it was my turn. I wanted to go on the Mega-Loop, of course! So we made our way over to it.

It looked even bigger and scarier when you were standing right underneath it! The queue was a bit longer than for some of the other rides, but it wasn't too bad. We went over to join the end of it – and you'll never guess what happened! Those creeps appeared again right behind us and pushed in again! We were so shocked, none of us could do anything about it, even me! We just stood and stared at them while they killed themselves laughing.

"Right, that's it!" I clenched my fists. "You're going to move this time or else!"

"Who's going to make us?" jeered Sticking-Out Ears.

"We are!" Frankie told him.

"Get off!" scoffed Ginger. "We're not afraid of five wimpy little girls!"

"What about *ten* girls?" said a familiar voice right behind us.

CHAPTER TWELVE

Surprised, we all looked round. Maria and the others were standing behind us in the queue, staring hard at the three boys.

"These are our friends," said Pilar. "So now we are *ten* girls!"

I stared at Maria. Then I moved next to her so that we were standing shoulder to shoulder. "Yeah, so you'd better move out of the way!" I said with a grin.

"We're not scared of ten girls!" said Ginger, although his two mates didn't look quite so sure. "We're not scared of a *hundred* girls!"

"Hey, I've got an idea!" Frankie announced.

"Why don't we grab them and *kiss* them to death!"

This time the three boys went quite pale.

"Yeah, good one, Frankie!" Lyndz agreed. "Then their mates will really take the mickey out of them!"

"Now wait a minute—" Ginger began, starting to back away.

"Let's get them!" I yelled. "Come on – kissy kissy!"

And we all rushed forward. The three boys panicked and ran for their lives, nearly tripping over in their eagerness to get away. We all had to hold each other up, we were laughing so much.

"Did you see the look on their faces?" Rosie gasped.

"They look like... like we going to beat them up!" Isabella giggled.

"I don't think we'll be seeing *them* again in a hurry!" said Frankie.

"Good – I would not like to kiss them!" Pilar laughed. "They are very ugly!"

After we'd stopped laughing, Maria and I

started shuffling our feet and looking a bit awkward. Everyone else was standing round waiting for us two to say something.

"Thanks for helping us out," I muttered at last.

"Is OK." Maria shrugged. "We want to go on Mega-Loop, and when we get here, we see you have problem."

"I thought the M&Ms didn't want to go on the Mega-Loop," Frankie said.

"We say goodbye to M&Ms," Maria muttered, looking even more embarrassed. "We – how you say – dump them!"

"They annoy us very much!" said Pilar with a grin. "They not want to go on *any* good rides!"

"Typical M&Ms!" I said. "They're right wimps!"

"Yes, you are right about them!" Maria said. "And we think maybe they *did* send those nasty emails!"

"They not like you at all!" Isabella added.

"Well, we don't like them either!" I said firmly.

"We forget everything now and have a good time, yes?" Maria looked at me.

"You bet!" I said, and I meant it!

Now that there was ten of us going on all the rides, everything was even better. The Mega-Loop was *wicked*! You got spun round upside-down so fast it made your teeth rattle inside your head! Fliss and Isabella both looked pretty green when we got off, and I felt just a little bit funny myself. After that we went into the Haunted House, and then to the Hall of Mirrors. That had those weird mirrors that give you really funny reflections, and we nearly died laughing when we looked at ourselves.

Then it was time to go to the picnic area and meet the others for lunch. Boy, I wish you could've seen the M&Ms' faces when the ten of us turned us laughing and chatting and being best mates. The Queen and the Goblin looked as if they were going to burst with rage!

We all stuffed ourselves silly, and then Mrs Weaver and the other teachers rounded everybody up and we went to watch some of the afternoon shows. There was a show with animals doing tricks, and one with acrobats, and afterwards we were allowed to go shopping. I got a cool blue baseball cap with *WonderLand is Wonderful!* written on it.

"I wish we didn't have to go home," Rosie said with a big yawn as we climbed on to the coach. "We didn't get to go on all the rides."

"But at least Maria and Kenny made friends at last!" Fliss added as we all filed down the coach. I sat next to Maria, Frankie sat next to Pilar, Rosie and Anna sat together and so did Lyndz and Elena and Fliss and Isabella.

"Hey, look at the M&Ms!" I nudged Maria. "They look like they've swallowed a wasp!"

The M&Ms had just got on the coach, and they were glaring at us. They found seats as far away from us as possible, and then turned their backs on us.

"I am glad we not have to be friends with them any more!" said Maria. "They are – how you say – a pain in the neck!"

"Definitely!" I agreed.

Although we were all pretty tired, the trip home was great. We showed each other what we'd bought, shared what was left of our packed lunches and played games.

"That was my best day ever!" Rosie sighed as the coach pulled into the school playground. We were a bit late getting back and all the other kids had already gone home.

"And tomorrow's the last day of term – even better!" Frankie added. "Then it's the summer holidays!"

"It's a real shame we can't play any tricks tomorrow though," I grumbled as we collected up our empty crisp packets and picked up our bags. "Mrs Poole's a real meanie!"

I was a bit surprised by what happened next. Maria stared at me with her mouth open as if I'd just told her the sky was about to fall on her head! She immediately jumped to her feet and began gabbling away in Spanish to Pilar, who was sitting behind her. Then the others started joining in.

"Hey, what's going on?" I asked.

"I set a trick for your teacher!" Maria said

breathlessly, looking worried. "In her table. When she opens the drawer, flour will fall out over her!"

We all stared at her. "You set a trap for Mrs Weaver?" Frankie said, eyes wide. "Why?"

"It was Emma's idea," Maria muttered, looking ashamed. "She say it will be good fun."

"Well, it's too late to do anything about it now," I said. "Anyway, Mrs W. won't know who's done it, so you'll be OK."

"No, you not understand!" Pilar looked worried too. "Emma say we have to blame *you*!"

"What do you mean?" I asked.

"She put two more bags of flour in your – how you say – locker, Kenny," Pilar explained. "Then Mrs Weaver think it is all your fault!"

"The nasty little ratbag!" I hissed furiously, bouncing right out of my seat. "Right, Emma Hughes is for it!"

"Never mind that now, Kenny!" Frankie said. "It's more important that we go into school and get rid of that booby-trap. Or you're dead tomorrow when Mrs Weaver gets flour all over her!"

"Yeah, she'll go ballistic and so will Mrs Poole!" Lyndz agreed.

"We get rid of it," said Maria. "I go into school now and do it."

"I come with you," Pilar told her.

"Come on, girls." Mrs Weaver was waiting impatiently at the front of the coach, glancing at her watch. "Off you go."

We looked up and realised that everyone else had got off and we were last. So we scrambled our stuff together, and hurried over to the door.

"Right, we're a bit late getting back, so hurry straight home or your parents might start getting worried." And Mrs Weaver started ushering us over to the playground gate.

"Miss, I have to go into school for something," Maria began, but Mrs Weaver shook her head.

"Sorry, Maria. Whatever it is it will have to wait until tomorrow."

"But, Miss, I have to go into school!" Maria insisted.

"And it's still open, Mrs Weaver," Frankie

pointed out. "The caretaker hasn't locked up yet."

"Yes, that's because the cleaners are here, and we don't want you getting in their way." Mrs Weaver stood by the gate and watched as we all reluctantly filed out. "Now make sure you go straight home."

We didn't have any choice. We walked down the road, staring gloomily at each other.

"So what are we going to do NOW?" Frankie asked.

CHAPTER THIRTEEN

"We've got to get into school somehow," I said grimly, "or tomorrow I'm going to be in the biggest trouble ever!"

"You might even get expelled!" Fliss wailed.

"Oh, thanks a lot!" I snapped.

"Shut up and let's think about this!" Frankie said, taking charge as usual. "Look, we've got to go home first, or our parents are going to start climbing the walls."

"I have to come back later," Maria decided. "In one hour, when the teachers go home."

"Is good idea," Pilar agreed. "I come with you."

124

"I'm coming too," I butted in, "'cos *I'm* the one who's going to be in deepest doom if Mrs W. gets covered in flour!"

"I'd better come as well then," Frankie said. "Someone's got to be there to control Kenny!"

"Cheek!" I said indignantly.

"I'm coming too then!" chorused Lyndz, Elena, Rosie and Anna together. Fliss and Isabella looked at each other, then they both nodded too.

"We can't *all* go!" I spluttered. "With ten of us creeping round the school, we're bound to get caught!"

"No, hang on, I've got an idea!" Frankie said thoughtfully. "We'll split up!"

"What difference will that make?" I asked impatiently.

"We'll split up and go into the school through different doors," Frankie explained. "Then, if anyone gets caught, at least someone else has got a chance of making it to our classroom!"

We all thought about that. It made sense.

"OK, so we'll meet back here in about an

hour," I said, checking my watch. "Then it's Operation Flourbag!"

"D'you think the school'll still be open?" Lyndz asked.

"I dunno," I said doubtfully. "How long does cleaning a school take?"

We all looked at each other. No-one had any idea.

"We'll just have to risk it," said Lyndz.

"Yeah," I muttered. "I just hope this plan works..." Because if it didn't, the last day of term was going to be ruined, I was going to be history, and the Queen and the Goblin would have the biggest laugh ever at our expense...

"Where are Pilar and Frankie?" I hissed, looking at my watch for the millionth time.

Everyone else had met up outside the school gates right on time, except for those two, and now we were all getting edgy. We'd all told our parents that we had to go back to school to collect something we'd forgotten – none of them had minded, 'cos we were allowed to stay out longer anyway now that it was light in the evenings.

"Let's go without them," Fliss suggested, her teeth chattering with nerves.

"No, give them a few more minutes," Lyndz said. "Look, the school's still open." We could see that some of the windows were still ajar, so it was obvious the caretaker hadn't locked up yet.

"The cleaners must still be in there." I glanced impatiently up the road again, and there were Pilar and Frankie racing towards us. "At last!"

"Sorry!" Frankie gasped. "My mum went shopping for baby clothes today and she wanted to show them all to us!"

"Is the school still open?" Pilar panted.

I nodded. "But we've got to be quick. The caretaker might start locking up any minute."

"What if Mr Coleman starts locking up while we're inside?" Fliss asked nervously.

"We will be shut in?" Isabella squeaked, looking scared.

"'Course we won't!" I said confidently. "We can easily climb out of one of the windows!

Now, let's get a move on!"

Quickly we divided ourselves up into three groups. Fliss and Maria and I were going in through the main entrance doors; Elena, Rosie and Anna were going round the back; and Frankie, Pilar, Isabella and Lyndz were taking the short route through one of the cloakrooms.

Silently we crept in through the playground gates. It was still daylight so we had to run for cover behind a wall, and wait there for a few seconds to make sure that the caretaker hadn't spotted us.

"OK, let's go for it!" I whispered. "Good luck – and I hope we all make it!"

"Just a sec!" Frankie grabbed my arm as I was about to shoot off with Fliss and Maria. "Look over there!"

Frankie was pointing at the teachers' car park. To our horror, it was still full of cars – *and Mrs Weaver's red Metro was there too.*

"The teachers are still here!" Fliss wailed. "I thought they'd have gone home by now!"

"What're they doing here?" I groaned.

"Ssh! Listen!" Elena held up her hand. We all listened hard – and in the distance we could just about hear a Spice Girls song playing very faintly. The windows of the staffroom were wide open, and the noise seemed to be coming from there.

"They must be having an end-of-term party!" Lyndz said.

"Oh, great!" I said. "And the staffroom's really close to our classroom!"

"We can't give up now," Rosie pointed out. "Anyway, they'll probably be too busy having a good time to hear us!"

"Rosie's right," said Frankie. "We've got to go for it!"

We all took a deep breath and started slapping each other on the backs and doing high fives, trying to make ourselves feel braver. Then we split up and set off.

"I'm scared!" Fliss moaned in my ear as the three of us hurried over to the main entrance. "What if we get caught?"

"We just say we forgot something and we came to get it," I replied. "Don't say anything about the flour!"

Fliss, Maria and I had the longest journey through the school to get to our classroom, but at first it wasn't too bad. We went through the Infants, and cut through the hall, and then we were in the corridor that led up to Mrs Weaver's room. The staffroom was at the end of the corridor, and although the door was shut, we could hear the sound of music and people laughing and talking.

"Quick!" I grabbed Fliss and Maria, and dragged them along with me towards the classroom. The door was slightly ajar, and we rushed in. To our relief, the others were already there.

"We all made it!" I exclaimed.

"Yeah, but let's get a move on!" Frankie whispered. "Maria's got to get rid of that flour!"

Maria was already standing by Mrs Weaver's table, pulling a big black bin bag out of her pocket.

"Stand back!" she said. She pulled the top drawer open a very little way, and slipped the black bag over it. Then she pulled it out further, and we saw a small puff of flour as it all disappeared neatly into the black bag – instead of over Mrs Weaver tomorrow!

"Hey, that was cool!" I said admiringly. "How did you set that up?"

"Not now, Kenny!" Fliss hissed. She and Isabella were the look-outs over by the door. "Come on, let's get out of here!"

"Don't forget the flour in Kenny's locker!" Lyndz reminded us. Lucky she remembered! Quickly I went across the room, and looked in my locker. It was empty except for a really old and smelly pair of trainers, an empty crisps bag – and two big packets of flour.

"Creeps!" I muttered angrily as I took the flour out. It weighed a ton. "What am I supposed to do with this now?" Then I grinned as I had a really fab idea. "Hey, guys, what do you think of this?"

But I didn't get a chance to tell them what I was planning to do because Fliss and Isabella suddenly jumped away from the door, and gasped in fright.

"What is it?" asked Elena.

"M-M-M-Mrs Weaver!" Fliss stuttered, looking absolutely terrified. "She's just come out of the staffroom, and she's coming this way!"

CHAPTER FOURTEEN

Everyone had a major panic. If Mrs Weaver came into the classroom, we'd had it because there was nowhere we could hide.

"Close the door, Fliss!" Frankie hissed. "*Quietly!*"

Fliss's hands were shaking so much she could hardly manage it, but she did it. Meanwhile the rest of us crawled under the tables and tried to make ourselves as small as possible. If Mrs Weaver went past the classroom we were OK. If she just glanced through the glass at the top of the door as she went by, we would *probably* be OK. But if

133

she opened the door and came in... we were dead meat.

I kept my eyes on the door. I saw Mrs Weaver's head appear in the glass at the top – and then she went by. I heaved an enormous sigh of relief.

"She's gone!"

"Let's get out of here then!" Fliss wailed.

"No, wait!" Frankie cut in. "It might be better to stay here till she's gone back to the staffroom. Otherwise there's a chance we might bump into her while we're trying to escape!"

We couldn't argue with that, although none of us were very keen on staying in the classroom a minute longer than we had to. But I had something to do before we left anyway.

"Kenny, what're you up to?" Frankie asked as I picked up the two bags of flour.

"Oh, just paying back the M&Ms for getting us into this mess!" I said cheerfully. "Maria, give me a hand, will you?"

*　*　*

134

Maria and I had just finished setting up our surprise for the M&Ms when Elena and Rosie, who were being look-outs, started waving madly at us.

"Mrs Weaver's coming back!" Rosie mouthed silently at us. We all dived under the tables, and waited. Mrs Weaver went past again, and then we heard the staffroom door open. A blast of noise came out.

"What's that!" Frankie gasped, covering her hands with her ears. "It's horrible!"

"It sounds like a dog howling!" Fliss added.

"No, it isn't." I started laughing. "It's Mr Coppins singing! The teachers are doing karaoke!"

We all started giggling and we had to stuff our hands in our mouths to muffle the sound. Rosie opened the door a bit wider so that we could hear it better. After Mr Coppins had finished murdering a Boyzone song, Mrs Weaver did a Madonna impression! We all nearly died laughing.

"Come on, let's get out of here!" Frankie said at last. "We've wasted enough time already!"

Still giggling, we tiptoed across the room, and peered out of the door. Luckily the staffroom door was closed, but the teachers were making so much noise, I don't think they'd have noticed if we'd dropped a bomb on them!

"Right, shall we split up again?" I whispered.

"Nah, no point," Frankie whispered back. "Let's just get out of here as fast as we can!"

We all ran down the corridor. We were nearly back at the main entrance, when suddenly Elena, who was at the front, stopped dead in her tracks, and the rest of us all bumped into each other as we skidded to a halt.

"I can hear noise!" Elena gasped. "Someone is outside!"

We all listened. She was right. There were definitely footsteps approaching!

"Quick, hide!" Frankie hissed, diving into a nearby classroom.

We all scattered. Isabella, Fliss and Rosie followed Frankie, while Lyndz, Anna and Pilar dashed into the hall. Maria, Elena and I raced into the Infants' cloakroom, and flattened ourselves against the wall.

The footsteps got louder. Someone was coming in through the door.

"Hello?" said a familiar voice, and I nearly dropped dead with fright! It was Mrs Poole, our headmistress! "Who's there?"

She'd heard us! I glanced at Maria and Elena, who both looked as scared as I was.

"I said, who's there?" Mrs Poole repeated. "You'd better come out, whoever you are!"

None of us moved.

"Right, I'll have to come and find you then!"

We heard the sound of heels tapping across the entrance hall – and they were coming in our direction! Mrs Poole was coming over to the cloakroom!

"What we do now?" Maria whispered urgently in my ear.

For once I didn't have a single bright idea. Mrs Poole was going to catch us red-handed, and there was nothing we could do about it. I just hoped the others kept quiet and managed to get out safely after we'd been captured...

"Betty! We've been waiting for you!"

That was Mrs Weaver's voice! I groaned silently. How many more teachers were we going to have to get past before we could escape?

"Oh, hello, Jane," Mrs Poole replied. "I was just wondering if some of the staff were lying in wait for me – you know, to play an end-of-term trick on me!"

"Not this time!" Mrs Weaver said with a laugh.

"Yes, I still remember last term when you turned all the furniture in my office upside-down!" Mrs Poole started to laugh too. "How's the party going?"

"Fine, but we're waiting for you to come and give us a song!"

"Right. Funny though, I could have sworn I heard someone moving around…" Mrs Poole was coming closer to the cloakroom. "Maybe we ought to check the classrooms."

I held my breath.

"Oh, come on, you're missing all the fun!" Mrs Weaver said firmly. "We'll ask the caretaker to look around if you're worried."

Mrs Weaver and Mrs Poole walked off down the corridor together. We waited till the sound of their voices had died away, and then we sneaked out of our various hiding-places.

"Did you hear *that*?" I asked indignantly. "The teachers are allowed to play tricks at the end of term, but we're not!"

"I didn't know the teachers behaved like this at the end of term!" Frankie grinned as we tiptoed out of the door. "I thought they spent all their time tidying the classrooms and moaning at us!"

"They'd die if they knew we'd heard them doing karaoke!" Rosie giggled.

It was still light when we got out into the playground, and we had to be careful making our way over to the gates. When the last one of us had finally dashed out, we all heaved a big sigh of relief.

"We made it!" I said triumphantly.

"Just about!" Frankie grinned. "Mrs Weaver nearly caught us a few times!"

"I've got to get home right now," Rosie said,

glancing at her watch. "I've got to finish off my fancy-dress costume for tomorrow."

"Me too," said Lyndz and Frankie together.

"Let's get out of here." I walked off up the road, and the others followed. "I've had enough of school to last me a lifetime!"

"This was all my fault," said Maria. "I am very sorry."

"Yes, if we did not listen to M&Ms, this would not happen," Pilar chimed in.

"No, it wasn't your fault," Frankie said, slapping her on the back. "This was all down to the M&Ms! They were the ones who started everything off by sending those emails!"

"Yeah, and tomorrow they're going to get exactly what they deserve!" I said with a big grin. "And I'm *really* looking forward to it!"

CHAPTER FIFTEEN

"Hey, Kenny!" The others were already waiting in the playground the following morning when my mum drove me and Maria to school. When they saw me, they all started laughing like drains.

"D'you want some help, Kenny?" called Frankie as I tried to climb out of the car. "You look like you're having problems!"

It was a bit hard getting out of a car with my mummy case on. I had my mask on top which was really big, and then the cardboard boxes Frankie and I had stuck together covered me from my neck almost down to my feet. Frankie and Lyndz had helped me to paint the boxes all over with hieroglyphics. Underneath I'd wrapped some bandages round myself too, so that I could burst out of the boxes just like a mummy in a horror film! I looked cool, even if I did say so myself!

"'Bye, girls!" My mum waited patiently until I'd managed to heave myself out of the car. Maria, who was dressed in her Real Madrid football strip, gave me a hand. "Have a good day."

"'Bye, *Mummy*!" I said and the others giggled.

"You look gruesome, Kenny!" said Fliss, who was just wearing a pink dress and a pink headband to match. It must have taken her all of thirty seconds to come up with *that* Barbie costume!

I stuck my arm out of one of the armholes in the side of the box. "Like my bandages?"

The others fell about.

"Hey, Maria, Kenny – guess what?" Rosie, who was dressed as a black and white cat and had a really fab mask with long whiskers, was nearly bursting with excitement. "I nagged my mum all evening yesterday, and she gave in and said we could have another sleepover at mine tonight!"

"Excellent!" I gasped. "An end-of-term sleepover!"

"And a goodbye sleepover because we go home tomorrow," Maria added.

"Let's have a really good one," Frankie said. "But no makeovers!"

I grinned and had a good look at everyone else's costume. Lyndz's Tin Man was brilliant! The silver paint she'd used was really shiny, and made the cardboard boxes look just like tin, and she'd made a wicked oil can as well.

"Can you guess who Elena is?" Lyndz asked.

I looked at Elena. She was wearing a blue dress with a white apron, and carrying a little basket with a stuffed dog sitting inside it. I didn't have a clue who she was meant to be – until I looked down and saw the red shoes she was wearing.

"Hey, you're Dorothy from *The Wizard of Oz* too!" I said.

Elena grinned and nodded.

"So what do you reckon, Kenny?" Frankie did a twirl so that I could see her *The Lion, The Witch and The Wardrobe* costume. It looked pretty good. It was a long dress all in white and silver, and she had a wand with a big glittery star at the end, silver make-up and silver nail varnish.

"Good one!" I nodded. Then I glanced at Anna who was all in green with a funny hat on her head. "What're you, Anna? A pixie?"

"What is pixie? No, I am Robin Hood!" Anna said, looking a bit put out. "I made a – how you say – a bow and arrow, but Maria sit on it and break it!"

"Sorry!" Maria said with a grin.

Isabella and Pilar looked pretty good too. Isabella was a butterfly, with big chiffon wings in bright colours, and Pilar was Mickey Mouse! She had the trousers and the white gloves, and she'd made herself some mouse ears out of some cardboard and a pair of black tights!

"I reckon one of us is bound to win a prize!" I said. "That'll be one in the eye for the M&Ms!"

144

"I'm not so sure about that!" Frankie nudged my mummy case. "Look over there…"

We all looked across the playground. The Queen and the Goblin were just getting out of Mrs Hughes' car. They were both dressed up like Victorian ladies, and they were wearing long dresses with big skirts and bonnets and high-heeled lace-up boots. Emma was carrying a lacy parasol and so was Emily. We all stood and stared at them, our mouths open. They *were* the Gruesome Twosome – but we had to admit they looked good.

"They didn't make those costumes themselves – no way!" I said angrily. "You're supposed to make the costume yourself to win a prize!"

"It looks like their parents have been slaving over those cozzies for weeks!" Frankie complained. "They're bound to win!"

"I do not think so!" said Maria, winking at me. "We have surprise for them, remember?"

That started us all giggling.

"Come along, girls, didn't you hear the bell?" Mrs Weaver came hurrying across the playground from the car park, looking a bit the worse for wear. She was dressed up as a clown in a baggy white suit and she had a big red nose stuck on too!

"You look good, Miss!" Frankie said, winking at the rest of us.

"Oh, thank you, Frankie." Mrs W. gave a huge yawn. "So do all of you!"

We all filed into class, having a good laugh when we saw what other people were wearing. I had to go in sideways so I could get my mummy case through the door! Ryan Scott was an alien, Danny McCloud was Dracula and other kids in our class were dressed up as a werewolf, a Teletubby, Superman and lots of other things.

"Mrs Weaver looked a bit sick, didn't she?" Frankie said with a grin. "Where is she anyway?"

"Probably gone up to the staffroom to take some aspirin!" I replied. "That was some wild party last night!"

At that moment the M&Ms swept into the room, holding up their dresses and looking snooty. We all started nudging each other and giggling.

"Hey, Emma, what're you and Emily meant to be then?" called Ryan Scott, looking puzzled.

"We're Victorian ladies, you wally!" Emma snorted.

"Bor-ing!" Ryan stuck his tongue out at her. "Why didn't you come as something decent?"

Emily glared at him. "You wait – Emily and I are going to win the prizes for best costume!" she snapped, as she rustled over to her locker. Emily followed her, and we all glanced at each other. Obviously we knew what was going to happen next, but we didn't want to give it away!

Emma reached out to open her locker.

"EEEK!" she roared as the booby-trapped bag of flour tipped over and showered her dress and face with white powder. Emily saw what had happened and tried to jump back out of the way, but it was too late. She'd already started opening her locker, and the same thing happened to her! They were both covered from head to toe!

"W-w-who— w-what—!" Emma spluttered, coughing as she got some flour in her mouth.

"Hey, Emma, you're not Victorian ladies now – you're ghosts!" yelled Ryan Scott, and the whole class collapsed into giggles.

"What on earth is all this noise about?" Mrs Weaver came into the room, yawning her head off – and nearly dropped down dead with shock when she saw the M&Ms covered in flour! "What's going on?"

"Someone put flour in our locker, Miss!" Emma coughed furiously, "and I bet I know who it was too!" She spun round and glared at us, and we all started laughing again. We couldn't help it – her face was completely white!

"Ryan, go and get Mr Coleman and ask him to clear up this mess," Mrs Weaver said briskly. Then she turned to stare at us with narrowed eyes. "Does anyone know anything about this? Francesca? Laura?"

"They must have set it up last night, Miss!" Emily Berryman roared, "after we got back from the theme park!"

"But we went straight home, Miss!" Frankie chimed in quickly. "You saw us!"

"Yes, that's true…" Mrs Weaver frowned. I reckon she *thought* it might be us, but she couldn't see how we'd done it.

"You must have done it this morning then, Kenny!" Emma snapped, still wiping flour off her face.

"What! Like this?" I looked down at my mummy case. "I can hardly move without someone helping me!"

"Well, one of the others must have done it then!" Emma yelled.

"We only got here a few minutes before the bell so we wouldn't have had time!" Rosie said.

"Well, it's certainly a mystery." Mrs Weaver stared hard at us, and we all looked innocently back at her. If she asked us right out if we'd set the trap, Maria and I would have to say yes. But unless she did, we were keeping quiet! "What a shame your costumes are ruined, Emma and Emily. They look very nice too. What I can see of them."

"I know you did this, Laura McKenzie!" the Queen hissed as the caretaker arrived to sweep up the flour. "And you're not going to get away with it!"

"Serves you right for sending those emails!" I hissed back, and Emma turned purple with rage. "Anyway, we got away with it before, didn't we!" And I waggled my mummy mask at her. "Remember this?"

Emma stalked off, trailing a cloud of flour, and she and Emily went off to the girls' loos to try and sponge their dresses clean.

"That was close!" Fliss muttered nervously. "Mrs Weaver looked dead suspicious!"

"I think she's too tired after the party to care very much!" Frankie grinned. "The M&Ms are crushed to bits – what a great way to end the summer term!"

"It's not quite finished yet," I reminded her. "We've still got the sleepover tonight!"

CHAPTER SIXTEEN

"I told you my mummy costume was cool!" I said triumphantly as we lay inside our sleeping-bags in the tent in Rosie's garden that evening. "Mrs Weaver thought it was ace!"

Lyndz and Pilar had won the prizes for best costumes in our class, and they'd got book tokens. But Mrs Weaver had said that mine was so unusual, she was giving me a Mars bar as a special prize! I was dead thrilled. I'd never won a prize for anything I'd made in my life before!

"Yeah, well done, Kenny!" said Frankie. "Now stop going on about it, will you!"

"I'm going to keep this Mars bar for ever and ever!" I announced, holding it up so that everyone could see it. "I'm never going to eat it, even if I'm starving! Is there any more chocolate left?"

Fliss sat up and searched through the empty packets lying around. "No, we've scoffed it all!"

"Oh, well!" I pulled the paper off the Mars bar and bit off a chunk. I passed it round, and in a few seconds it had disappeared.

"Did you see the M&Ms' faces when we won the prizes?" Frankie giggled. "They were so furious they had steam coming out of their ears!"

"What?" asked Pilar, looking puzzled.

"Not really!" Frankie told her.

"They are your big enemies now," Elena said seriously. "You must be careful."

"Oh, we can handle the M&Ms!" I said, screwing the Mars wrapper up and flicking it at Fliss. "They don't scare *us*!"

It had been a brilliant sleepover so far. Lyndz had brought her little brothers' paddling-pool with her, and we'd blown it up and filled it with water, and then we'd spent ages jumping in and out of it, splashing each other. It was too small for us, but that was part of the fun! Then we all tried getting in it together – it was a real laugh! After that we'd played International Gladiators, and then Rosie's mum had come out and told us it was time for bed, so we'd all crawled into the tent. Maria had pulled the tent flap back so that we could see outside, and now we were lying in rows, looking up at the stars as it got dark.

"This has been the best end of term ever," Fliss said sleepily.

"And the bestest sleepover ever," Rosie added.

"And this has been my best holiday ever in my life," Elena said solemnly.

"I think so too," Anna agreed. "And you are our best friends."

"And you're our best friends!" Lyndz told her.

"And Leicester City are the best football team in the world!" I said.

"No, they're not – Real Madrid are the best!" And Maria kicked me through the sleeping-bag.

"Oh, shut up, you two!" Frankie groaned. "Don't start a football argument!"

"Shall we sing our Sleepover song?" Lyndz asked.

"Wait till I get back." I climbed out of my sleeping-bag and winked at Maria. We had something else in mind – one last trick before the Spanish girls went home tomorrow! "I've just got to nip to the loo."

"Me too." Maria got up and followed me out of the tent. Then we hid behind a tree and waited, trying not to laugh.

We could hear Lyndz humming our Sleepover song – "Down by the river there's a hanky-panky…" And then we heard her say "Poo! What's that smell!"

Maria and I nudged each other and doubled up with silent laughter.

"Urrgh! It's horrible!" That was Fliss.

"It smell very bad!" squealed Isabella.

"It's Kenny and Maria!" Frankie yelled.

"They've let off a stinkbomb!"

Next second all eight of them were fighting to get out of the tent, and flapping their hands in front of their noses. Maria and I just couldn't keep quiet any longer – we hung on to each other and laughed out heads off!

"Right – let's get them!" Frankie roared, and the others grabbed their pillows and chased us right round the garden.

So we ended up having a fight on the last day of the visit just like we'd had on the first day – but this time it wasn't for real! It was just a good laugh.

It was really sad saying goodbye to our mates the next day, but at least we've got the summer holidays to look forward to. We're going to have lots of sleepovers, but from now on I'm going to keep out of trouble! No, don't laugh – I mean it!

Oh-oh, got to go. Molly the Monster's just got back from camp, and I've got an ace trick to play on her. I'm going to let my pet rat Merlin curl up and go to sleep on her bed – that'll freak her out! See you later!

Sleepover Girls on the Catwalk

Brown Owl has arranged for the Cuddington Brownies to put on a show for the local old people's home. Fliss is determined to make it a fashion show, but the rest of the Sleepover gang have other ideas... Will everything go to plan, or will there be catwalk chaos?

Pack up your sleepover kit and strut your stuff!

www.fireandwater.com

Visit the book lover's website

The Sleepover Club Goes for Goal!

Kenny joins the school five-a-side football team and manages to bore her friends stupid about it... that is, until the Sleepover Club form a team of their own! What a good excuse for a special football-themed sleepover...

Get your footy boots on and head for the pitch!

www.fireandwater.com
Visit the book lover's website

22

The Sleepover Club go Babysitting

Baby Morgan needs a babysitter urgently, and the Sleepover girls kindly agree to take charge. After all, what can be difficult about looking after a little baby? But things are never that simple for Frankie and friends – that's what makes life so crazy!

Pack up those nappies and toddle on over!

www.fireandwater.com
Visit the book lover's website

Order Form

To order direct from the publishers, just make a list of the titles you want and fill in the form below:

Name ....

Address ....

....

....

Send to: Dept 6, HarperCollins Publishers Ltd, Westerhill Road, Bishopbriggs, Glasgow G64 2QT.

Please enclose a cheque or postal order to the value of the cover price, plus:

UK & BFPO: Add £1.00 for the first book, and 25p per copy for each additional book ordered.

Overseas and Eire: Add £2.95 service charge. Books will be sent by surface mail but quotes for airmail despatch will be given on request.

A 24-hour telephone ordering service is available to holders of Visa, MasterCard, Amex or Switch cards on 0141- 772 2281.

Collins
An *Imprint* of HarperCollins*Publishers*